THE TRIUMPH OF FOLLY

It should have been easy for Annabel Wyndham to choose between the two men who vied for her hand.

One was a lord whose very name bore the aura of scandal— Sir Charles Norbury, a picture of male attractiveness, a fashion plate of elegance, and a man whose touch seemed to melt her very soul.

Her other suitor was the most honorable, kindly and generous-spirited man she had ever known—Christopher Hanford, who promised her his honest love, her children a stepfather they already adored, and her future serenity and security.

It should have been easy for Annabel to choose between these two—as long as she chose with her clever head instead of her foolish heart. . . .

FIRST SEASON

SIGNET Regency Romances You'll Want to Read

FIRST SEASON

by
Jane Ashford

A SIGNET BOOK
NEW AMERICAN LIBRARY

NAL BOOKS ARE AVAILABLE AT QUANTITY DISCOUNTS WHEN
USED TO PROMOTE PRODUCTS OR SERVICES. FOR INFORMATION
PLEASE WRITE TO PREMIUM MARKETING DIVISION, THE
NEW AMERICAN LIBRARY, INC., 1633 BROADWAY, NEW YORK,
NEW YORK 10019.

SIGNET TRADEMARK REG. U.S. PAT. OFF. AND FOREIGN COUNTRIES
REGISTERED TRADEMARK—MARCA REGISTRADA
HECHO EN CHICAGO, U.S.A.

SIGNET, SIGNET CLASSIC, MENTOR, PLUME, MERIDIAN AND NAL BOOKS
are published by The New American Library, Inc.,
1633 Broadway, New York, New York 10019

First Printing, January, 1984

1   2   3   4   5   6   7   8   9

PRINTED IN THE UNITED STATES OF AMERICA

Chapter One

"Well, I don't like it here," said Nicholas Wyndham, looking around the elegantly furnished blue drawing room with a jaundiced eye. There was nothing obviously offensive in the delicately molded white ceiling, the thick Turkey carpet, or the fashionable French tables and sofas, but his brother, Sir William, the elder by a year, seemed to concur. He grimaced sympathetically and shrugged. "We must do something!"

"But, Nicky, what could we possibly do?" William's deep blue eyes widened.

Nicholas sighed. He and his brother looked much alike, resembling their mother in soft brown hair, pale coloring, and fine bone structure. And William was a splendid fellow for a tramp through the woods or a wild gallop, neck or nothing, behind the local hounds. But Nicky often felt that their father's heir lacked some quality that he himself possessed in abundance. "Scores of things!" he retorted, drumming his slender fingers on his knee and considering.

Sir William Wyndham, very conscious of his responsibility as head of the family, sat straighter in the blue velvet armchair and shook his head. "Now, Nicky, don't begin one of your high flights."

His brother snorted. "You've been pleased enough with some of them. What about Mr. Winston?"

William grinned. Mr. Winston, a late and unlamented tutor in the Wyndham household, had left it precipitously. "That was Susan, not you."

"It was my idea to set her on him."

"Yes, but . . ."

"Well, I admit that Susan is enough for anyone."

As the brothers pondered this truism, in perfect agreement, the subject of it came hurtling through the double doors that led to the hall, leaving them standing open behind her. "Here you are!" She stood, hands on hips, green eyes smoldering. "I suppose you thought I shouldn't find you here?"

They eyed her warily. Susan Wyndham, the youngest of the family, had inherited a mass of flaming red hair from her paternal forebears and an irresistible temper from sources unknown. Her brothers had long since learned to respect her opinions. "We thought you were busy upstairs," ventured Nick.

"You didn't! How could I be, in this beastly place? I hate it here." Coming farther into the room, she subsided into the armchair opposite William with a flurry of white muslin skirts.

"All of us do," agreed William, putting his chin in his hand.

"Well, we should go back home, then," replied his sister. "Let us speak to Mama at once." She made as if to rise.

William laughed shortly, and Nicholas said, "Mama is out. And, besides, she likes it. I heard her say so."

Susan's auburn brows came together, and her full lower lip began to protrude. Both brothers braced themselves.

But before she could gather voice for an initial blast, there was a soft sound from the doorway and then a scraping noise from behind the sofa where Nicholas sat. "Daisy?" wondered Susan.

"Oh, no." William sprang up and shut the doors. "Is he scratching the table? Nicky, look and see."

Reluctantly, Nicholas peered over the sofa back, directly into the yellow eyes of an immense ginger tomcat, who had sunk his front claws into the scrolled leg of a Louis Seize table. Holding the boy's gaze, the cat bent slowly forward and fastened his teeth on the same object. Nicholas shuddered and drew back. "Yes."

"Get him!" William ran around the sofa.

"Daisy!" shrieked Susan, leaping to the rescue. The cat streaked under the couch, coming out directly under Nicky's feet and causing him to jerk them up convulsively.

"Come on," shouted William. "We'll corner him."

His brother swallowed and rose, squaring his shoulders. "I'm coming." He moved forward like a soldier going into battle.

"No," cried Susan. She ran over and scooped the animal into her arms, his oversized body drooping on all sides. "Leave her alone!"

William sighed again. "Him, Susan. I keep telling you. I can't understand why you had to drag that horrid creature off the streets. You might have had a kitten of your own if you'd asked, and not some wretched alley cat."

"She was starving," replied Susan with finality, caressing Daisy's flat head. The cat purred but continued to stare at the Wyndham brothers with malicious glee.

William gazed at the gigantic animal skeptically, but merely shrugged. Nicholas shuddered again and turned away.

"Daisy can help us," added Susan, lugging him back to the armchair and settling him across her lap.

"Help us what?" asked William.

"Get home again." Susan's dimples showed. "Cook doesn't like her."

"None of the servants do," agreed Nick, in a tone that suggested he was wholeheartedly of their opinion.

"Yes." Susan smiled again.

"That don't signify." William was superior. "They'll simply get rid of the cat. They wouldn't . . ."

His sister's green eyes flashed, and she drew herself up. "I should like to see them try!"

"Yes, but, Susan—"

"This isn't getting us anywhere," interrupted Nick. "We have to decide what we're going to do. I can't bear it much longer." He glanced at Daisy.

"Nor I," agreed Susan. "London is the dreariest place I've ever been."

"Well, I can't see what we . . ." began William, but at that moment the drawing-room doors opened again to reveal two ladies in modish evening dress.

"Whatever am I to do with her, Anabel?" the elder was saying. "She . . ." They saw the Wyndhams.

"What are you doing downstairs at this hour?" exclaimed the other woman. "Why aren't you getting into bed?"

"We were just talking, Mama," replied Sir William Wyndham, full of the maturity of his ten years. "I was about to take the children up."

His brother's lip curled.

"I don't want to go to bed," protested Susan, six. "Nor does Daisy." She held up the cat's head so that her mother and grandmother could see it over the chair arm. "*She's* not the least sleepy."

Both women looked pained. "I daresay not," answered Lady Anabel Wyndham. "But you must go up." She sent

8

a footman in the hall to fetch Nurse, who arrived a few moments later in a confusion of starched white and protests that she had been searching for the children throughout the upper floors. "That is no doubt why they came down here," responded their mother, shepherding the three toward the stairs.

"Will you come up and say good night?" begged nine-year-old Nicholas.

"In a little while, if you get into bed."

Susan grimaced, but they went.

"Really, Anabel," said Lady Sybil Goring when they had the drawing room to themselves. "Shouldn't the boys be in school? They aren't a very good influence on Susan, apparently."

Anabel laughed. "I assure you it is quite the other way about, Mother. But you're right, they should go. I have been trying to bring myself to send them for a year." She shook her head.

"I'm sure they've been a great comfort. But, Anabel, it has been three years since Ralph died."

"I know." She looked down again and sighed. "It doesn't seem so long."

Her mother watched her with pity and some impatience. She had married Anabel off very young to a most eligible baronet, and she had thought her well and happily settled until the untimely death of Sir Ralph Wyndham three years before. At that tragedy, she had understood and respected her daughter's grief, allowing her every indulgence in her power and taking care not to manage her life, as she had been greatly tempted to do. Lady Goring's powerful common sense quite often led her to intervene in her friends' and family's decisions. But now she thought it was time Anabel shook off her despondence and began again. She was, after all, not yet thirty, and she did not look the least like the mother of three growing children.

Indeed, with her soft brown ringlets, large, expressive blue eyes, and delicately made frame, Anabel could have passed for a girl of twenty. Only her mother knew that her fragility was deceptive: Anabel might look as if a strong wind would carry her away, but she had great reserves of strength.

Accordingly, Sybil had swept her daughter up to London for the season, over her protests, and she was determined that its gaieties should dispel the last clouds of bereavement. Her only concern was the children, whom Anabel had insisted upon bringing. They seemed out of spirits in town, and their unhappiness was the one thing that might spur Anabel to open rebellion. "I was wrong to let your father convince me to marry you without a come-out," she murmured. She did not realize that she had spoken aloud until Anabel looked up, smiled, and shook her head.

"I didn't mind, Mama."

"That is because you knew no better. You had no taste of town life, and you still have not. You don't know what you missed."

"I know what I gained." Anabel smiled reminiscently.

Her mother ignored her. "But we shall make up for that now. You shall go to all the balls and entertainments just as if it were your debut, only you will enjoy them a great deal more because you have the freedom of a married woman." As soon as she said this, she wished she hadn't, but Anabel merely shook her head again.

"I am too old for a debut."

"Wait until you have gone about a bit before you decide."

"This ball tonight . . ."

"Oh, it is not a ball. A trial before the season really begins, nothing more. You must not go by it."

"Mama." Anabel smiled. "Content yourself with managing Georgina. I shall stay in the background."

"Nonsense," snapped Lady Goring, but this brought back her earlier grievance. "Anabel, what am I to do about Georgina? I'm sure when I told your uncle that I would bring her out I was happy to help. He hasn't been up from the country since Clara died, fifteen years ago. But now that I have seen her . . ." She made a helpless gesture.

"What precisely is wrong with her?" asked Anabel, who had not yet met her much younger cousin. "She arrived this afternoon?"

"While you were shopping."

"Is she coming down to dinner?"

"I suppose so. I mean, I should count on it." She laughed bitterly.

"Mama . . ."

A footman opened the double doors to admit a girl of seventeen or eighteen to the drawing room, and Anabel saw at once what her mother had meant. Georgina Goring possessed an altogether too ample abundance of flesh. Her frame went well beyond youthful plumpness, and as if to call attention to the unfortunate flaw in her appearance, she entered eating a large cream-filled chocolate.

"Georgina, dear," murmured Lady Goring in a faint voice.

"Hullo," replied Georgina around the candy. "Is it dinnertime?"

Anabel bit her lower lip.

"Nearly, dear. This is your cousin Anabel. My daughter, you know."

"Hullo," said Georgina again. "Are you coming out this season, too?"

Her smile broadened. "In a manner of speaking."

Georgina nodded. "You will do better than I. It is all so stupid. I don't see why I need bother." She took a twist of silver paper from the pocket of her pink muslin gown, extracted another chocolate, and ate it.

Lady Goring made a stifled noise. "You won't care for any dinner, will you, Georgina, if you keep eating sweets."

"Oh, yes, I shall."

Anabel looked from one to the other. Perhaps this visit to town would be more amusing than she had expected. When her mother had first insisted that she come to London, she had refused. For three years her life had revolved around her children, and before that she had become accustomed to living in the country. She had neighbors to rely on for company and aid, and she knew her family loved the outdoors. But her mother had overborne her objections, holding out the lures of excitement and change. Anabel had been tempted, she knew, and she had also realized that her children needed her less and less with each passing year. The boys should go to school, and Susan was nothing if not independent. She had consented half reluctantly, but now her lively sense of the absurd was aroused by the contest of wills she saw shaping before her, and she felt the first stirrings of gratitude. She had been feeling a bit old and weary lately. Perhaps her mother was right.

She glanced from the older woman to Georgina again. She knew her mother's strength of purpose, only too well, but something in Georgina's expression suggested that Lady Goring might have met her match. The girl seemed both stubborn and not particularly concerned with Lady Goring's opinion. Surveying her, Anabel realized that she was not really unattractive. Though undoubtedly fleshy, she had fine pale blond hair and gray eyes with thick dark lashes. Her hands were lovely. Turning, Anabel met her mother's gaze, and her lips twitched. It was compounded of chagrin and a dawning fanatical determination.

"Dinner is served, madam," said the butler from the doorway. Georgina followed him eagerly into the hall.

"You see?" said Lady Goring in a low voice.

"She is a little plump. From the way you were talking, I expected a hunchback at least."

"A *little?* Annabel!"

"Well, Mama . . ."

"You may think it a good joke, but I have promised to bring the girl out and find her a husband, if possible, of course. Her fortune is only moderate; I had hoped she would be pretty. If only the current fashions were more flattering to . . . but these waists, and no lacing at all." She shook her head. "Chocolates! How can she?"

Anabel started toward the door. Georgina would be wondering what had become of them.

Her mother's chin came up as she turned to follow. "I have two weeks before the season officially begins," she finished. "I'm sure a great deal can be accomplished in that time. She must come with us tonight, but it is a mere hop. Hardly anyone will be there."

"Perhaps we needn't go, then," replied Anabel mischievously as they walked down the corridor.

"Anabel! Don't you begin now, or I shall certainly go distracted."

"You, Mama?"

"Indeed I shall. If anyone had told me that I should sponsor the first seasons of a thirty-year-old woman and an absolutely . . . massive schoolgirl, I should unhesitatingly have pronounced them mad."

Anabel began to laugh. "Not *quite* thirty, Mama."

"How can you be so unfeeling?" Lady Goring met her daughter's dancing eyes and started to smile. Linking arms with her, she strode into the dining room, where Georgina was already seated and looking impatient. "Amuse yourself while you may," she concluded. "I shall triumph in the end—wait and see."

Chapter Two

It was fortunate, thought Anabel as the three of them descended from the carriage at the front door of the Rivingtons' festively lit town house, that this ball was not one of the great events of the season. Neither Georgina nor Lady Goring was in the best of tempers after wrangling throughout dinner over what the girl should or should not eat. Indeed, Anabel herself had started to feel the strain of the contest of wills before she thought to remind her mother of the time. Georgina had not spoken once during the short journey, and Lady Goring's comments, though general, had retained an acerbic tone. Anabel was very glad to give her wrap to a footman and climb the stairs to greet her hostess. She would avoid her family until the entertainment put them in better frame, she decided.

The ballroom was more crowded than she had expected, and the hum of talk and glitter of evening dress abruptly reminded Anabel that she loved parties. She had scarcely attended one since her husband died, at first because she was in mourning and then because she had somehow gotten out of the habit. Now she felt a rising excitement.

London parties must be quite different from the dinners and small assemblies of the country. She had told her mother that she hadn't minded missing her long-ago debut, but she remembered now that this wasn't entirely true. She had pined a little for the balls and routs and Venetian breakfasts until she became so contented with Ralph and the children.

"Lady Wyndham," said a voice behind her. "I didn't know you were in town."

Anabel turned and greeted a woman she had met some time ago at a house party. "Mrs. Brandon, how pleasant to see you again." She would have an easier time now than she would have had at eighteen, she realized. There were one or two familiar faces in the room.

When they had exchanged commonplace news, Mrs. Brandon added, "You must come and meet my daughter. It is her first appearance in society, and she is naturally a bit uneasy. She will be so happy to see an acquaintance."

Glancing around, Anabel saw that her mother and Georgina were lingering near the door, the former scanning the crowd and the latter looking remarkably sulky. "I should be delighted," she replied, and allowed herself to be led to the other side of the broad chamber.

It was evident at once that Julia Brandon had no memory of meeting her and that she was by no means pleased to see either of them. A tall, Junoesque brunette, as Mrs. Brandon must have been before putting on flesh, Julia was talking to a gentleman when they came up, and her irritation at the interruption was almost as clear as her mother's anxiety. Anabel surveyed him with interest and some amusement. What about the man inspired such disparate emotions in mother and daughter?

Part of the answer was obvious immediately. He was extremely handsome. Julia Brandon's height had made her companion's less evident from a distance. Now, looking up, Anabel felt dwarfed. The two women outstripped her own moderate inches, but the man was taller still, and he held himself with a consummate assurance. His hair and coloring were dark, and he was blessed with the fine shoulders and well-molded leg to set off the high Corinthian mode he affected. Though Anabel had never lived in town, even she could recognize the elegance of his dark blue coat and fawn pantaloons, the one chaste fob dangling at the front of a severely unostentatious waistcoat. Here was an example of the nonpareils she had only heard of. Anabel was suddenly acutely aware of the outmoded cut of her evening dress. Her mother had assured her that it was fine enough for this early ball, but she wished now that some of the London gowns she had ordered had arrived to replace her old blue satin.

Raising her eyes, she looked into the man's face. The high cheekbones, broad forehead, and dark arched brows matched the rest of his appearance. His mouth looked haughty, she thought. And then she met his gaze.

Anabel felt a shock run through her, from her throat to the pit of her stomach, leaving her shaken and absolutely astonished.

The man's eyes were a curious pale green, and they reflected a masterful and complex personality. That was clear at a glance. But why should they affect her so strongly?

Mrs. Brandon had murmured her daughter's name and Anabel's. Now she added, "Sir Charles Norbury," in a voice thick with disapproval and concern. She had moved close to Julia's side, and her stance made it clear that nothing would move her until she could coax the girl away.

Anabel saw in Norbury's eyes an appreciation of the situation that matched her own. A silent current of amusement passed between them. "Wyndham," he said. "I knew a Julian Wyndham at Oxford."

"My husband's cousin," replied Anabel.

"Ah." There was a subtle shift in his gaze.

"My dear Lady Wyndham," exclaimed Mrs. Brandon. "I did not even mention your sad loss. I beg your pardon. It was such a shock, Sir Ralph going off that way. Julia was much affected, weren't you, dear?"

Julia, whose entire attention remained on Norbury, didn't appear to hear.

"You are very kind," replied Anabel. "It has been three years now, and so we are over it, as much as we ever shall be." Mrs. Brandon nodded sympathetically, and Anabel was a little surprised to realize that this now-familiar platitude was quite true. In the country, with her family and surrounded by objects that recalled Ralph, she had not really felt the fading of grief. Here it was clearer.

"Oh, Julia, there is Maria Kingsley, and her daughter, I believe. Come, we must speak to them." She took Julia's arm and urged her away. "You will excuse us?"

Their murmured responses, and Julia's frown, were swept aside in Mrs. Brandon's determined retreat. Anabel wondered again why she was so eager to get away.

"My fault, I'm afraid," said Sir Charles Norbury.

"I beg your pardon?"

"The abrupt departure. I'm not considered a proper companion for young girls just out of the schoolroom." He smiled, teeth startlingly white against his dark skin. "Thank God."

Anabel couldn't help smiling back, though she was startled by his apparent reading of her thoughts and by his remarks.

"Why not?" she couldn't resist asking.

He laughed a little. "I'll leave it to others to malign my character, I think. Will you dance?"

The ball had opened in a rather disorganized way as they talked, and now a new set was forming. Anabel, intrigued, nodded and put a hand on his arm. She was a little disconcerted to find that it was a waltz.

"You haven't been up to London before," said Norbury when they were circling the floor together.

"No. We always preferred the country." It seemed to Anabel that he was disturbingly close. She had waltzed at local assemblies countless times, but somehow this was different. Norbury's arm about her waist and firm clasp of her hand seemed to make it a new experience, and she felt foolishly younger than her years.

"Really?" He treated it as a joke, and Anabel was too preoccupied with her own odd sensations to correct him. "But you must have spent at least one season here. Perhaps we even met? Yes, I must have danced with you. My taste has always been impeccable." He smiled down at her, his light green eyes glinting.

"No. I married out of the schoolroom." She felt it a clumsy reply, and was again amazed at herself. What was making her so inept? Ralph had always called her a wit.

"That accounts for it, then." Sir Charles was still smiling.

"For what?"

"You are quite the youngest and loveliest widow I have ever encountered, Lady Wyndham."

"Widow," she echoed distastefully. "How I hate that word. It makes one think of . . ."

"Precisely. But you confound all the clichés delightfully."

Anabel had never met anyone who anticipated her in this way. It had always been she who surprised and amused her circle, her conversation that set the standard. She was slightly stung at being interrupted, but even more she was interested and challenged. "And you? Do you *not* go to Jackson's, and Manton's Gallery, and White's, and the Daffy Club?"

"Not?" There was an arrested look, and a shade of puzzlement, in his eyes.

"Clichés." She left him to work it out, which he soon did, throwing back his head in a laugh so genuine and wholehearted that several nearby couples turned to look.

"A leveler, Lady Wyndham! Or perhaps I should say a telling comment, not wishing to betray my lamentable lack of originality. How dare you hide in the country all this time when you might have enlivened the desert of society with such home thrusts?"

"Ungallant, sir. Not *all* this time," she answered, looking demure.

He didn't laugh again, but the spark of delight remained in his eyes. "I most humbly beg your pardon." He guided her in a sudden turn, his arm tensing around her, and Anabel drew in her breath. This was the most stimulating conversation she could remember.

"You *are* here for the season, I hope," he added. "Have you taken a house?"

"No, I am staying with my mother, Lady Goring."

"Ah. Yes, we are acquainted. I hope you will allow me to call upon you there?"

Anabel inclined her head.

"In fact, as this is your first extended visit to London, perhaps you would allow me to show you some of our landmarks. The park at the fashionable hour is well worth seeing. Will you go driving with me tomorrow?"

"In a high-perch phaeton?" she asked.

He laughed again. "In anything you like, my dear Lady Wyndham. A Roman chariot, a stagecoach complete with yard of tin."

She smiled speculatively up at him, then shook her head. "I should like to ride in a phaeton."

"Letting me off so easily?"

"Oh, no. I shouldn't like being stared at in a stagecoach on Rotten Row."

"But that is the chief object in London—being stared at."

"In a particular way. Not with ridicule."

"Indeed. But many do not see the distinction." The music ended, and Sir Charles looked disappointed. "Tomorrow, then?"

Anabel nodded, and they drew apart with the end of the set. She felt both glad and sorry that it was over. It had been exhilarating but also a little overwhelming. She looked around for her mother and discovered her standing in the doorway that led to the refreshment room. Norbury offered his arm. "May I get you something?"

They walked across to Lady Goring, who greeted them with raised eyebrows and turned to join their progress. "I have hardly seen anyone," she replied to Anabel's question. "I have spent most of the evening in here." She sounded so irritated that Anabel and Norbury exchanged a glance. But Anabel had a suspicion of the cause, confirmed when she saw Georgina standing close to the buffet table, alone.

They joined her, and Anabel made introductions. Neither Sir Charles nor Georgina appeared enthusiastic about meeting.

"Georgina, darling," said Lady Goring. "You really must come into the ballroom. Everyone is still dancing." Her voice was oversweet, and her eyes rested on the plate of lobster patties and meringues in Georgina's hand.

Georgina shrugged and took a bite of meringue.

Anabel struggled with a smile. She looked at Norbury to see if he shared her amusement, but he was eyeing Georgina with a mixture of weariness and disgust. His mouth had turned down, and his lowered lids eloquently expressed contempt. Anabel felt uneasy about what he might say.

"Georgina," said Lady Goring again, sharply. "This is a ball, not a dinner party. No one else is—"

Anabel felt she had to intervene. "How are the meringues?" she asked, then grimaced. That was hardly the question to ease the situation.

Georgina looked at her. "All right."

This effectively halted the conversation. Lady Goring had become aware of her audience. Sir Charles looked bored. "If you will excuse me," he said, "I see Allingham." With a careless nod, he walked away.

"You had an ample dinner only two hours ago," Lady Goring said to Georgina more quietly. "I wonder you can eat anything."

"I am excessively fond of meringues," responded the girl defiantly, taking another bite.

"Excessively indeed." Lady Goring was uncharacteristically cutting.

Anabel couldn't bear any more. "Mama, I think Mrs. Rivington was looking for you. She wanted to ask you something."

"Me? What could she possibly . . ."

"I don't know. Perhaps you should go and see."

Her mother eyed her suspiciously, then sighed. "Very well, Anabel, I shall go. But I must say first that I am not pleased by your choice of a partner."

"My . . ."

"Norbury, my dear. I didn't know you had met him."

"I was introduced here."

"I see. Well, it is too bad, but I suppose you can avoid him in future."

"Why?"

Casting a meaningful glance at Georgina, Lady Goring turned to go. "We will discuss it later."

Anabel frowned at her back. Really, her mother was becoming more managing rather than less so with age. She had been almost unkind to Georgina, and now she evidently thought to dictate her own friendships. She would have to realize that Anabel was no longer a schoolroom miss. She turned back to Georgina, who was finishing a meringue. Their eyes met.

"You don't have to stay here with me," said Georgina. "I am quite happy alone."

Nonplussed, Anabel watched her pick up another confection.

"I prefer it, actually," added the other.

"At a ball?" Anabel could not help but ask.

Georgina shrugged. "I don't care for balls. I hate crowds of people."

"But . . . the season."

"I shall hate it. I knew I would. I never wanted to come to London, but Papa insisted. We were quite happy at home together, and then last year he suddenly began to talk of London and of writing my aunt. He wouldn't listen to me at all."

Anabel noticed incipient tears in the girl's eyes. "I'm sure he thought it would be best for you."

"How could he? He knows I loathed the assemblies and evening parties he made me go to at home. *He* hates them, too. He never goes out. We are just alike, Papa and I." The tears threatened to overflow, and she blinked them back furiously.

"What do you do at home?" asked Anabel gently.

"We read. We both love books. And we have very good dinners. Our cook is French. And no one tells me that I should look better in my ball gown if I did not eat my dinner. And no one is forced to dance with me when he does not wish to." Georgina sniffed and ate another meringue.

"Perhaps your father was thinking of the future," offered Anabel. She was feeling a great deal of sympathy for her cousin and wanted to comfort her.

22

"I am his only heir," replied Georgina bluntly. "I will have the house and an adequate income. He has told me."

"Well . . . but you should have a family of your own and . . ."

"Why? I don't want one." The girl sounded both defiant and unhappy.

Anabel did not know just what to say to her. On the one hand, her mother was right. If Georgina would do something about her appearance, she would no doubt have a pleasanter time in London. But she realized now that what she had taken for sullen stubbornness in Georgina was in reality a mask for bewilderment and hurt. Perhaps some young man had been rude to her this evening, and certainly Lady Goring's criticisms had wounded her. She was striking back by refusing to change, and she had some justification. Anabel did not know what she could do for her, but kindness was surely better than further humiliation. "What sort of books do you like?" she asked.

Georgina's gray eyes brightened a little. "Novels. Do you read them?"

"I have little time for reading, I'm afraid. I seem to be always busy with the children."

She nodded, accepting this. "Are you glad you came to London?" she asked. "You like it here, don't you?"

"Well, yes. I do enjoy parties." Anabel felt almost apologetic.

"You are pretty. Everyone likes you."

She laughed. "Hardly."

Georgina shrugged again. "That man you were dancing with does, and he didn't even want to look at me."

So she had noticed Norbury's reaction. Anabel had hoped she had not. She tried to think of some reassuring answer.

"It's all right. I don't care. I am perfectly happy the way I am." Georgina picked up another meringue.

But Anabel, watching her, knew that it wasn't true, and she wondered again what she could do for her touchy young cousin. The girl couldn't be pushed; that was clear. Was there some more subtle means of aid? No thoughts occurred to Anabel, and the musicians were striking up another waltz in the ballroom, drawing her irresistibly away. Dancing again had been wonderful.

"Go ahead," said Georgina.

Anabel hesitated, then turned toward the music. She would think about her cousin tomorrow.

Chapter Three

Anabel enjoyed herself hugely at the ball, and as a consequence slept luxuriously late the following morning, waking barely in time to dress for her appointment with Sir Charles Norbury. Thus, she was not downstairs to receive a morning caller who asked for her with some impatience. Indeed, no one was about, and the footman left the gentleman in the drawing room to go in search of Lady Goring.

The man paced the elegant room in long, swift strides, obviously preoccupied. Once, thinking he heard a sound, he stopped and turned quickly. But no one was there. He was dressed in well-tailored traveling clothes, though not in the height of fashion, and there was something very appealing in his ruddy blond complexion and alert blue eyes. He was just above medium height and just past thirty years of age, and his handsome face fell naturally into lines that suggested laughter.

Still pacing, this time he did not hear the faint noise from the doorway. But it was followed almost immediately by a shriek that brought him swinging around.

"Uncle Christopher!" A diminutive figure hurled itself

across the carpet and onto his chest, nearly knocking the breath out of him. "You're back, you're back!"

"Hello, Susan," he replied, hugging her like a man accustomed to such assaults. "I am. I arrived this morning."

"How did you know where we were?" Susan had drawn back a little and was pulling him toward the sofa, where she settled herself on his knee.

"I saw it in the newspaper."

The child's green eyes went wide. "Are we in the newspaper?"

"Your mother is. It says she attended a ball last night." His tone in imparting this information was ambiguous.

"Oh. That." Susan's interest vanished. "I am so glad to see you, Uncle Christopher. You must take us all home at once."

Christopher Hanford eyed the small girl meditatively. He was not really her uncle. The Wyndhams and the Hanfords had been neighbors in Hertfordshire for generations, and he had grown up with Ralph Wyndham and remained his closest friend even after the latter's marriage. Upon his untimely death, Hanford had naturally become the mainstay of Wyndham's bereft young family, and all of the children called him "uncle." Anabel, too, relied on him. He had always been happy to oblige. But in the last six months or so he had gradually realized that his happiness was not simply that of a faithful friend. The Wyndhams had less and less need of him as the grief for Ralph faded and Anabel learned about running an estate and managing alone. Yet he called as often and found himself resenting the change. Finally the truth had struck him. He had, in the past three years, fallen deeply in love with his charming neighbor, and he could no longer be content without her.

This knowledge had unsettled him, chiefly because Anabel herself showed no signs of returning his regard. She was always glad to see him and treated him with the relaxed informality of long-standing friendship; she seemed delighted by his love for her children. But on the few occasions when he had tried to express more profound feelings, she had not understood, or perhaps, as he sometimes thought, she had pretended not to, thinking he would see that she could offer him nothing more. This conclusion had so cast him down that he embarked on a sudden voyage abroad, resolving to stay away until he had conquered his unrequited passion. He told the Wyndhams only that he was leaving, and he did not write. But this accomplished no more than to keep him wondering how they were through the entire trip. Last week he had given it up and turned homeward, determined to confront Anabel and find out his chances. But almost the first thing that greeted him in England was the announcement that she had brought her family to town. He was irrationally angry that she should have taken this step without consulting him, and uneasy about its consequences.

"Have you seen her?" asked Susan, tugging at his lapel to get his attention. "Uncle Christopher!"

"What? Seen whom?"

"Daisy. My cat. I'm looking for her. She comes down here all the time, and the servants get angry."

"I haven't seen her, Susan. I'm sorry."

Susan shrugged and smiled angelically up at him. Not for the first time, Hanford marveled at the strange combination of seraphic face and hellish temper.

The drawing-room door opened again, and Nicholas peered around it. When he saw Hanford, he looked first astonished, then delighted. "William!" he called over his shoulder. "Here." Then he in his turn ran forward and embraced the man, to be followed quickly by the elder male Wyndham. "How good that you are back," said

Nicholas when their greetings were over. "You can speak to Mama."

Hanford smiled at his assurance. "About what?"

"Going home, of course. I daresay she will be more willing to go now that you will be there."

"What makes you think so?" he replied rather sharply.

"Oh, things were dreadfully flat after you went. We all said so."

"Your mother, too?"

This time Nicholas glanced up at his eagerness, slightly puzzled. "Oh, yes. Will you tell her? We dislike London so." William and Susan nodded vigorously.

"We shall see." He felt a rising hope. Was it possible that Anabel had come to London because she missed his company?

The footman opened the door and ushered Lady Goring in. Hanford put Susan aside and rose to greet her. But before either could speak, a large mass of ginger fur streaked past her ladyship's feet, almost oversetting her, and buried itself in one of the blue velvet draperies. It was hotly pursued by another footman, who arrested his headlong rush barely in time to avoid his employer. He came to attention, breathing hard and pulling at his coat to adjust it, just outside the room.

"Whatever is the . . ." began Lady Goring, then stopped and sighed. "The cat again, I suppose."

"Yes, ma'am," answered the footman. "He got into the kitchen, and Cook says—"

"Susan, you promised me you would keep that animal upstairs," interrupted the other, not wanting to hear what Cook had said. She could easily imagine it.

"I *did*, Grandmama. Only, Miss Tate said I had to do my lessons, and so I—"

"I know you want to keep him, Susan. But he is really not the sort of pet for you to . . ."

Seeing Susan's ominously reddening face, Hanford ventured, "I believe he is climbing the curtain."

He was. William and the footman ran to the window, followed more slowly by Nicholas. The cat's progress was evident only from a moving agitation of the cloth, but he was already above the reach of the brawny footman. "A chair," suggested Hanford, and one was quickly shifted. Daisy was retrieved with an ominous rip and a flurry of claws and teeth. Susan ran to cradle him.

"Go downstairs and have Mrs. Beecham tie up your hand at once, James," said Lady Goring in a long-suffering voice. The footman, hands behind his back to hide the bleeding, hurried away. "Susan!"

"Daisy was just frightened. She didn't know what they were going to do to her, did you, Daisy?"

The giant cat focused a derisive yellow eye on the group.

"If he cannot be kept upstairs, Susan . . ."

"I will. I will, Grandmama. I promise!"

Lady Goring sighed. "We will try it once more. But only once, Susan. Do you understand me?"

"Yes, Grandmama." She gripped Daisy more tightly, his tail, legs, and belly hanging over her small arms. The cat surveyed his audience complacently.

Lady Goring stepped forward, holding out her hand. "I beg your pardon for this uproar. I am Anabel's mother, and though we have not met, I have heard a great deal about you. I am delighted to make your acquaintance at last."

Hanford bowed slightly as he took her hand. "And I yours." His bright blue eyes were still dancing at the scene he had just witnessed, and Lady Goring found herself smiling.

"Shall we sit down?"

They had hardly done so when the unwounded footman

came in again, announcing, "Sir Charles Norbury," and ushering that gentleman into the room.

There was an immediate alteration in the atmosphere. The tall, very fashionable figure who strode to the middle of the carpet and looked down at them was in marked contrast to the inhabitants of the household. Lady Goring was well dressed, but common sense rather than changing modes always governed her choices. Christopher Hanford was a countryman, and his clothes, although good, had no pretensions to elegance. In his many-caped driving coat and gleaming Hessian boots, Norbury seemed to epitomize the town buck, and his sardonic expression as he scanned each of them merely increased this impression. "Good day, Lady Goring," he said. "I hope I do not . . . intrude?"

Hanford disliked him at once, for no discernible reason. And Lady Goring's reply was not warm. She implied, without actually asking, a question about his visit.

"I am here to fetch Lady Wyndham for a drive in the park," he said. "Did she not mention it to you?" His slight smile and one raised brow were very handsome, and extremely annoying to his adult listeners. Hanford's dislike was confirmed, and joined by suspicion. Lady Goring frowned. Their visitor appeared amused.

"I want to go, too," stated Susan, putting Daisy down on the floor. "Mama said we might go to the park, but Nurse never wants to take us."

Norbury eyed her with distaste, and Lady Goring recalled her duties as hostess with a certain relish. "You haven't met my grandchildren, Sir Charles," she said cordially. She gave their names. William and Nicholas made very creditable bows, but Susan merely moved closer to the man and stared up at him with a fixity that earned her a haughty look. "And forgive me, Mr. Hanford, I ought to have mentioned you first. Mr. Hanford is a neighbor of my daughter's in Hertfordshire."

"I see." Sir Charles was obviously impatient. "I fear I cannot keep my horses standing too long, Lady Goring. If Lady Wyndham might be informed of my arrival . . ."

"Oh, John has gone to tell her. I daresay she will be right down." She seated herself and indicated with a gesture that the gentlemen should follow suit.

Daisy had been scouting the perimeters of the room since being set free, and now he looked out from under the sofa, drawn by the high shine of Norbury's boots. Nicholas, under whose legs the cat emerged, drew them quickly up. Daisy stepped out, head extended, and sniffed delicately. The sound attracted Sir Charles' attention, and the sight of Daisy brought a twist to his lips. Some instinct made the cat raise its head and meet the man's pale green gaze. In an instant the streetwise creature had retreated out of sight.

"You have been traveling abroad, Mr. Hanford?" said Lady Goring.

"Yes. I've only just returned."

"How did you find the Continent now that the war is over? Much changed?"

"Well, I had never visited it before, so I am not the person to say. But it is certainly interesting."

Norbury's face showed contempt at this commonplace, and Hanford, who had replied at random as he tried to work out what he would say to Anabel when she appeared, felt a strong desire to hit him.

"My husband and I visited Paris on our wedding journey," said Lady Goring. "We always meant to return, but the war came, and then Gerald's death, and we never managed it. Paris is a wonderful city."

Hanford agreed. Sir Charles hardly tried to conceal his impatience.

William and Nicholas had effaced themselves since the

second caller arrived, feeling that their presence was now unwelcome, at least to him. But Susan was unhampered by such scruples. She had wandered to the window and now she approached Norbury's chair. "Is that your carriage outside?"

"Yes."

"I've never seen one like that. What is it called?"

He looked annoyed. "A high-perch phaeton." His voice was clipped.

"Why is it so tall?"

Alarmed by Sir Charles' languid annoyance, Lady Goring and Christopher Hanford spoke at the same moment.

"That is the fashion," she said.

"You can see a great distance from the seat," he said.

They glanced at each other, smiled slightly, and apologized. Norbury looked pained.

"But . . ." Susan was never easily diverted.

"I am so sorry I am late," exclaimed a breathless voice from the doorway, and Anabel hurried in, looking charming in a white sprig muslin gown, with tiny blue flowers and long tucked sleeves, and a chip straw hat. She carried a dark blue pelisse over her arm.

The gentlemen stood, Norbury stepping forward.

"Christopher!"

"Hullo, Anabel."

"When did you get back?"

"Just this morning." She had come forward and offered her hand, and he took it and squeezed it warmly. The way her face had lit when she saw him had speeded his pulse.

"However did you find us so soon?"

"You were in all the society papers."

"I?" She seemed both astonished and a little pleased.

"Yes, indeed. 'The charming Lady Wyndham.' " His eyes teased her.

"Oh, my."

"I beg your pardon," put in Sir Charles, "but I really cannot leave my horses standing much longer."

Anabel turned quickly. "Indeed, it is my fault. I am sorry." She looked back at Hanford, biting her lip. "We must go."

He said nothing. He refused to tell her it was all right.

"Are you staying in town long, Christopher?"

"A few days." He had planned to go straight home, but her presence changed that.

"Good. I will see you later, then. Good-bye Mama, children."

"I want to go with you," said Susan. "You promised I could see the park."

"Nurse will take you this afternoon, dear."

"I want to go now!"

Seeing Norbury's face and knowing her daughter, Anabel cravenly fled with a hurried "Another time, love." Lady Goring, watching the youngest Wyndham's imperiousness turn to outrage, braced herself. William and Nicholas waited with identical grimaces.

"The park is very dull at this time of day," said Christopher Hanford. "I know a better place. Have you heard of Astley's Amphitheatre?"

"Where they have the wild beasts?" asked William.

"That's it. Why don't we have a look at it today?"

The boys leaped up and began to pelt him with questions, their exuberance revived. Hanford kept one eye on Susan. At first it seemed that she would cling to her grievance. But when William's hope that there might be lions was confirmed, she gave in and joined the group. Lady Goring, amazed and grateful, watched the exchange with a smile, then saw them all off in a hansom cab. As Hanford was bidding her good-bye she said, "I hope we shall have an opportunity to talk again, in better circumstances. Will you come to dinner one night?"

"I should be delighted."

"Tomorrow? We are at home."

He agreed and, as the children were clamoring to go, stepped up into the carriage. Lady Goring saw them off before turning back into the front hall, a meditative look on her face.

Chapter Four

Christopher Hanford was so punctual for his dinner appointment the following evening that he arrived before either Lady Goring or Anabel had come downstairs. As the footman took him to the drawing room to await them, Hanford felt unexpectedly awkward. He had purchased several new coats in Paris, having been assured by one of the best tailors that they became him and were in the very latest mode. He wore one tonight, but he had an uneasy suspicion that he could not compete with Sir Charles Norbury in this area. He looked like a sensible, well-bred gentleman, one whose family had been prominent in the county for centuries, but he was no Corinthian, and he never would be. Walking through the door the footman held open for him, Hanford again told himself that it was very common for ladies to be taken driving in town. It meant nothing in particular. Anabel could not be well acquainted with Norbury after such a short stay; perhaps she had merely gone out of politeness or the desire for variety. But he found his arguments unconvincing. The image of the polished Norbury had lingered painfully in his thoughts through the night, and his expression as he crossed the Turkey carpet toward the fireplace was wry and concerned.

"Oh!" said a female voice. There was a scuffling sound and then a cascade of small objects over the sofa front.

"I beg your pardon," said Hanford, moving around it. "The footman did not tell me there was anyone here."

Georgina Goring scrambled up. She had been reclining on the sofa, wholly engrossed in a book and fortified with a box of chocolate creams. The story was so enthralling that she had not heard the door open, and not until Hanford's footsteps were quite close had she noticed him. Startled, she had jumped, overturning the confections and raining them in confusion on the rug. Her heart was pounding because she had at first thought the intruder was Lady Goring, and braced herself for a scold. Discovering her mistake, she felt both embarrassed and irritated at facing a stranger and a male. "You crept up on me," she accused.

Hanford eyed the very plump pale girl with some amusement. The scene told him a great deal. "Indeed, I did not mean to. The servant did not say you were here."

"He didn't know," admitted Georgina. She had formed the habit of slipping about the house, so that Lady Goring would have difficulty in finding her and preventing her pleasures.

Hanford knelt and began to pick up the scattered chocolates. He handed her the book that had fallen facedown on the floor. "*The Monk's Curse*," he read. "Is that a novel?"

"Yes." She snatched it from him.

"Are you fond of novels?" He deftly returned the last candies to their paper holders and put on the box's cover.

"Yes." Georgina rose, taking this also from him and

36

clutching both to her. She was a trifle disheveled, and her gray eyes sparked defensively.

"So is my sister. She is continually telling me to read one or another, but I fear I am not a great reader. What do *you* like about them?"

The girl surveyed him suspiciously but could find no trace of mockery in his face. She thawed a little. "The stories are so exciting. I always feel as if I were hurtling down a long dark tunnel with no notion of what is to come next."

Hanford was surprised. The girl looked dull, but she was obviously not. "Do you? It sounds too terrifying for me." He smiled at her to show that he was joking.

Georgina gazed at him with wonder and dawning interest. No gentleman but her father had ever bothered to be kind to her before. And this was a very attractive gentleman.

"I am Christopher Hanford, by the way."

"Oh, no!"

He raised his eyebrows, still smiling.

"I beg your pardon. But you are coming to dinner."

"I am."

"I mean, you are here for dinner, and I have not changed. I did not hear the bell. My aunt will be angry with me. I must go at once before she comes down." But even as she hurried toward the door, still awkwardly grasping her possessions, it opened and Lady Goring came in, impressive in silver-gray satin.

"Georgina, what are you doing?" Her ladyship's sharp gaze took in the morning dress, the book, the box of chocolates, and her lips turned down.

"I was just going to change!" The girl almost ran past her and out of the room.

Lady Goring sighed heavily, then moved toward Hanford. "Good evening. I see you have met my niece."

"Yes. A very intelligent girl. I fear I startled her when I came in."

"No doubt she thought it was me. Sit down, please." They sat. "Georgina and I do not agree on a number of things." She noticed a lone chocolate, which had rolled under an armchair, and bent to pick it up. "Why will the wretched girl persist in eating candy? I am losing all patience with her! Can she not see that . . ." Remembering her company, she stopped.

"I daresay chocolates are what she has learned to love," replied Hanford, feeling some obscure kinship with Georgina Goring.

Lady Goring stared at him, and he felt a little sorry for his comment. "Anabel has told me that you are an extremely perceptive counselor. You have helped her with the children more than once, I know. It is for Georgina's own sake that I wish her to keep away from chocolates and the like. She will be much happier in London if she does."

He nodded. "It probably seems a criticism, however."

"What am I to do?" wailed his hostess. "I cannot manage Georgina, and here is Anabel mad after a notorious rake. I had no idea when I asked her to visit that—"

"Norbury?" he snapped.

Once again aware that she had said too much, Lady Goring bit her lip. "I don't know what it is about you, but I am letting slip things I would not say to anyone else. Yes, Norbury is not the sort of man any mother would approve."

"And she is 'mad after him'?"

Something in his tone made Lady Goring look up sharply. What she saw in Hanford's face narrowed her eyes. "I exaggerate. Anabel is merely intrigued."

"As yet." Her words had filled him with a disappointment so sharp that he had difficulty breathing normally. It would be unbearable if he were to lose Anabel in this way, to such a man.

"I daresay it is a passing whim. She was never exposed to town life, and she is finding it interesting."

"Interesting!" The tone was so bitter that Lady Goring's suspicion turned to certainty. She catalogued Hanford with care. From what she had seen, he was just the man for her daughter.

The door opened again, and Anabel came in. She was wearing a soft blue evening dress tonight that emphasized the size and color of her eyes. Her brown hair was dressed in a knot at the top of her head, with curls falling over her ears, where tiny sapphires sparkled. She came forward holding out her hand with undisguised pleasure. "Christopher. How good to see you again. You were away such an age."

He took it, feeling his throat tighten, and bowed slightly. "It seemed long to be away from my friends," he agreed.

"Oh, I'm sure you were having far too fine a time to think of us." She laughed. "Was it splendid?" She gazed up at him, her eyes shining with open happiness and affection. It really *was* wonderful to see him again, she realized. She had missed him more than she knew.

The others, watching her closely, felt varying degrees of satisfaction. Lady Goring was confirmed in her resolve, and Hanford felt stirrings of hope, though the image of Sir Charles Norbury lingered in the back of his mind. "My journey was pleasant, but I did indeed think of you. In fact, I have some things for the children I would like to bring."

"Presents. You spoil them so, Christopher." Anabel spoke teasingly, knowing that it wasn't true. He had been an unimpeachable substitute father since Ralph's death. They smiled at each other warmly over this old joke.

The group settled on the sofa and armchairs. "Are the

children in bed?" asked Hanford. "I hoped to see them again."

"Yes." Anabel threw a mischievous glance at her mother, who grimaced. "They had an active day, and we sent them off early."

"Active!" Lady Goring's tone spoke volumes, and Anabel laughed.

"You invited them, Mama."

"Yes, dear, and I love them all. But I had forgotten how wearing young children can be. I am happy to have them here and also happy when it is time for them to go to bed." Her comical grimace made them all laugh, and Georgina Goring entered the room to general merriment.

The footman was right behind her, announcing dinner, and they went into the dining room in very good humor.

It was the most enjoyable meal Anabel could remember in London. Her mother and Georgina did not quarrel at all. Once, it appeared they might begin, but Christopher somehow smoothed over the contretemps and turned the conversation with an amusing anecdote. They talked of the Continent, Lady Goring reminiscing movingly, and then, surprisingly, of novels. Georgina became almost animated. By the time they went back to the drawing room for coffee, Hanford seemed as much an old family friend to the Gorings as to Anabel. Lady Goring was amazed by the ease with which he adapted to them, and very much bucked up by his charm and endearing smile. Anabel seemed to glow in his presence as her mother had not seen her do in years. As for Georgina, she simply thought Christopher Hanford the most wonderful man she had ever met, perhaps surpassing even her beloved father.

When they had drunk their coffee and the footman had come in twice to put fresh logs on the fire, Lady Goring rose to her feet. "Georgina," she said, "I have something to show you in my room."

The girl looked surprised, then concerned. "Just now?"

"Yes, dear, come along." Lady Goring tried to convey with a look her desire to let Anabel and Hanford have a little private talk, but Georgina was oblivious.

"Can we not do it tomorrow?" Georgina had been having a wonderful time; she did not want it to end.

"No, dear." The older woman moved toward the door, beckoning.

Georgina's brow puckered resentfully.

"Come along."

She looked for support, but the others were talking. Sullen again, she rose and followed her aunt slowly from the room.

Anabel looked up in surprise when the door shut. "Where are they going?"

Hanford, who had seen and been humorously grateful for Lady Goring's maneuvers, shrugged.

"Well, it is fortunate. We can have a comfortable talk." Anabel smiled at him, and his heart turned over.

"Yes. You are enjoying London?"

"I am. I did not think I would at first, but I am beginning to realize that I had shut myself away too much."

This sounded ominous. "What made you decide to come up for the season?"

She smiled again. "Mama. Need you ask? I was feeling very flat at home, and she leaped at the chance."

"Flat?"

"Yes. I do not know how it is, but this summer seemed horridly dull."

Hanford hoped again. He had been away for the whole summer. "The children must be enjoying themselves. There are so many new things to see."

"They enjoyed Astley's," she answered with a grimace. "I must thank you again for taking them there. I hadn't thought of it, nor did Mama, of course. They have not been overly pleased with London until now. Your promises of future treats altered their view somewhat."

"My father first brought me to town when I was about Nick's age and showed me all the sights. I remember the trip vividly to this day."

Anabel held out a hand and, when he took it, squeezed his. "Thank you, Christopher. I can always count on you. I don't know what we have done to deserve such a friend."

He almost spoke then. He had opened his mouth to tell her what she had done when Anabel continued, "I was too taken up with my own pleasure to provide for theirs. Have you ridden in the park at the fashionable hour, Christopher? I have never seen such a spectacle."

The image of Norbury rose before him. He dropped her hand and sat back. "I'm told it is amazing."

"So many human types. And Sir Charles knew them all, of course, and could tell me their histories. I don't know when I have laughed so much."

"You like this Norbury?" He hadn't meant to mention him, but the question slipped out.

"I have never met anyone like him. He is . . ." Anabel tried to formulate an opinion while Christopher watched her narrowly. She had had a fine time on their drive the previous day. It had been a bit strained at first. Sir Charles had seemed annoyed, perhaps at having been kept waiting. But when they had begun talking, Anabel had again felt that nervous excitement he had aroused when they met. Sir Charles was certainly intelligent as well as handsome. His sketches of fashionable London had been hilarious, and it was obvious to Anabel that he was held in high esteem. Many people had greeted them, and others had looked and commented. She had been very conscious of her position beside one of the most elegant men in town. ". . . interesting," she finished, a bit lamely.

"I see."

She looked up, surprised at the dryness of his tone. "You do not like him?"

"I? I have hardly spoken one word to him."

"I know, but . . . Mama has the absurd notion that he is not . . . oh, never mind, Christopher. As if I could not take care of myself by this time." Anabel laughed, her glance encouraging him to join her. But Hanford, convinced that she was far from able to take care of herself, remained serious, his lips turned down. After a moment Anabel's smile faded. She was puzzled. Christopher had always been the first to savor a good joke. Surveying him, she saw worry in his face. His bright blue eyes were shadowed. What was wrong? Knowing his love of the country, she thought that he might be missing his home. "When do you return to Hertfordshire?" she asked. "You will find everything much the same there, though Mrs. Petty has managed to wrest the Poor Committee from old Mrs. Duncan at last."

This made him smile a little. "Has she indeed? But I am not certain I shall go down at once."

"Really? Why not?"

"I am thinking of staying in town for part of the season." His eyes gauged her reaction to this.

"You, Christopher? I cannot imagine you here."

This stung. "Some would have said that of you only a few months ago."

Anabel smiled. "That's true. But do you mean to join the season and make the rounds of parties and all that? You dislike parties so."

"No doubt the London festivities are more amusing than those in the country." His tone was a little clipped. He was angry at the implied comparison with Sir Charles, who was perfectly at home in town.

Anabel eyed him curiously. "Well, I can only marvel at

43

this change. I have heard you swear you would never be caught in London during the season."

"Perhaps I have changed my mind." He was very annoyed with her now. Could any woman really be so blind? *She* was here, so he would stay, however much he disliked parties. Surely the connection was obvious?

Light seemed to dawn on Anabel. "I have it! How foolish I was not to see it at once."

He looked at her.

"You have decided to marry at last, and you have come to town to find a wife." She laughed up at him.

This was too much. He merely stared at the floor, lips set.

"*Is* that it, Christopher?" She sounded both surprised and not completely pleased. "I was only funning." His continuing silence daunted her. Could this really be his reason? She had never pictured Christopher marrying, though of course nothing would be more natural, she realized. He ought to marry. But when she tried to imagine it, to think what sort of woman would be best, Anabel felt a sudden, unaccountable rush of annoyance. She tried to explain it to herself. Christopher might have informed her of his plans. They were, after all, old friends. And how would the children feel at the intrusion of a stranger into their familiar circle? They would not understand, particularly when Christopher began to desert them for his own prospective family. He might have prepared her for this, so that she could prepare them. But it was all of a piece. He had gone abroad with hardly more than a word, and now he meant to alter their old, comfortable relationship in the same way. It was really unkind. Her surge of emotion satisfactorily explained, Anabel raised her head and met his eyes, her softer blue ones hot.

Hanford, who had been watching her expression shift, was cautiously elated. She had not at all liked the notion of his marrying, he saw. Well, then, perhaps he would let her consider it further. She might even discover that her feelings for him were not simple friendship and that she herself wished to fill the position of his wife. Accordingly, he merely shrugged in response to her questioning look.

Anabel was outraged. She had confidently expected a laughing denial and she felt cheated and deceived. Christopher had never said one word about marriage through the years of their friendship. Clearly, she was not really in his confidence; he had no respect for her opinion at all. Anabel rose. "It is late."

"I beg your pardon. I shall take my leave of you, then." Hanford had some trouble controlling a smile. He was very pleased with her reaction.

Chin high, she held out her hand. "I daresay we shall see you at some of the season's events."

"No doubt," he agreed amiably.

"I hope you do not find them tedious after all."

"Anabel, I think that extremely unlikely." Now he did smile, and she, interpreting it as anticipation of the courting ritual, pulled away her hand and stepped back. Hanford left the room with a jaunty salute and a lingering smile.

Chapter Five

As a result of this conversation, Christopher Hanford paid a rather early morning call the following day, to a small but very elegant town house in Regent Street. Mrs. Amelia Lanforth appeared astonished when he followed the butler into her drawing room. "Christopher? Are you still in London? I was sure you would be safely in Hertfordshire by this time, tramping about your muddy fields."

"I have decided to stay in town for a while, Amelia."

She gaped at him. The two were remarkably alike, both just above medium size with ruddy blond hair and bright blue eyes, but Mrs. Lanforth's tresses were fashionably curled à la Méduse, and her pink muslin morning gown had obviously come from one of the most skillful London modistes. "Is something wrong?"

"No."

"It must be. You needn't spare me, Christopher. Is it Aunt Seraphina? She wasn't at all well the last time I called, but—"

"Nothing is wrong. Can I not spend a few weeks in town without arousing this astonishment?"

She looked at him again. "No, you cannot. You have not voluntarily visited London for more than two nights since you were twelve years old, Christopher. Come to that, you have never called on me more than once in a visit since we settled here. And you have repeatedly told me how silly I was to enjoy town life. *What* is wrong?"

Hanford gazed down at his sister with a wry smile. She was, of course, perfectly right. And if he wanted her help, he was going to have to provide some explanations. He and Amelia had disagreed on a number of things during their lives. From a very early age he had devoted himself to the estate and country amusements, whereas she had counted the moments until her London debut. She had reveled in her first season and married a man who habitually came up for that period, returning home only for occasional holidays and to be with their mother for the births of Amelia's two children. After the older Hanfords died, she ceased these visits, and she and Christopher now saw each other only a day or two each year, when he was in town. Yet strong bonds of affection remained between them despite this separation. Their disagreements had never been acrimonious; indeed, they almost enjoyed arguing their divergent points of view. Christopher had no doubt his sister would do as he asked, after she had twitted him over his change of heart. His expression became more wry. "I want to be a man of fashion, Amelia. Will you oversee the transformation?"

Her mouth dropped open. "You're bamming me!"

"Word of honor."

"But . . . but . . ."

Her amazement was so comical that he laughed.

"Christopher! You have nothing but contempt for 'men of fashion,' even poor Lanforth, who is far from a pink of the *ton*. What has suddenly changed your mind?" Before he could reply, her blue eyes sharpened. "A woman, I suppose."

He looked down.

"I had received the impression that you were interested only in your neighbor, Lady . . . oh. She is in London this season, is she not?"

"Have you met her at last?"

"No, but I remember hearing that Lady Goring has her daughter with her. This is your reason, then?" Her eyes had started to dance.

Sheepishly Hanford admitted it. "She is much taken with town ways and . . ."

"And town beaux, I suppose. Oh, Christopher, I could not have hoped for such a perfect revenge if I had planned it for years. You see where your country stubbornness has brought you." She was laughing almost too hard to speak.

"To throw myself on your tender mercies," he agreed. "I am in your hands, Amelia. Will you help me?"

"I wouldn't miss it for anything." She thought of something. "But you must do as I say, Christopher. No contemptuous sputterings."

He sighed but nodded.

"What fun I shall have!" She walked slowly around him, as if making notes.

"I have rather given Anabel the impression that I am hunting for a wife," he added.

"As you are. Oh, you mean among the debs?" Amelia's delighted smile returned. "How devious of you, Christopher. This may be easier than I thought. You have the instincts of a tulip already." As he grimaced she continued. "First, you must get rid of that coat. You should never wear olive drab, with your coloring. It is cut well enough, but . . ."

"I bought this coat in Paris," he protested.

"And I said it was well enough. But the color is all

wrong. You should always wear blue, or buff or black, but never olive."

"But it was—"

"Christopher! You promised you would do as I say."

Their very similar eyes met. "Very well," he muttered.

"Good." Amelia smiled. "We must get you a new haircut, of course. And your cravat will never do. Oh, Christopher, we shall have such fun!" She clapped her hands gleefully. Her brother grimaced again. "Are you still at Claridge's? I will send someone for your things." Seeing him start to speak, she added, "You must stay here, naturally. It is one thing to claim you will give me too much trouble on a one-night visit to town—which is ridiculous, as I have always told you. But if we are to carry through your plan, you cannot be so far off. You can have the blue bedchamber. It's all ready."

Hanford watched her animated features as she set forth an arduous program of shopping for the next several days. He had rarely seen his sister so pleased. It made him glad he had sought her help, though he knew he would not enjoy much of it. If anyone could prepare him to compete with Norbury, it was Amelia, and he was determined to do everything in his power to win in this unforeseen contest.

The first major event of the season was the Duchess of Rutland's ball the following week. Amelia had no trouble securing an invitation for her brother, and she hounded his tailors so mercilessly that he was completely reoutfitted in plenty of time. As he came into the drawing room that evening both Lanforths turned to look at him, Amelia with a professional's critical eye and her husband, George, with a combination of fellow feeling and curiosity. He, too, had been a victim of his brother-in-law's mockery of the *ton*.

Christopher felt ridiculous. His new clothes seemed outlandishly exaggerated, despite his sister's assurances that both cut and fabric were very plain. His hair, cut and brushed into a Brutus by a fellow he had found intolerable, seemed stiff and strange. And he was almost frightened of the valet Amelia had made him hire to care for his new finery. "Here I am," he declared, stopping beside them. "Complete with cap and bells."

"You look splendid," encouraged George. "Top of the trees."

"You have left off your quizzing glass," objected Amelia. "I told you, it is to hang—"

"I *could* not," he interrupted. "I have tried my best to be docile, Amelia, but I simply could not."

Meeting his gaze, she smiled a little. "Oh, very well. You *do* look splendid, Christopher. Even I did not imagine that you could look so polished." She eyed his black evening coat and knee breeches, his snowy cravat tied in an Osbaldeston, his silver-shot waistcoat. "Indeed, I would hardly have known you for my country-squire brother."

"I hardly know myself," he replied ruefully. "I glance into a mirror and start to nod to the overdressed stranger."

"Nonsense. You are not the least overdressed. Shall we go in to dinner? We do not want to be late."

"Do we not?" murmured Christopher. But he took her proffered arm and led her into the dining room.

Only a few streets away, the ladies of the Goring household were putting the finishing touches on ball gowns and toilettes before also sitting down to dinner. Anabel, surveying her reflection in a full-length glass, was very pleased with the effect of the ball gown that had arrived yesterday from her dressmaker. It was of deep blue satin with an overskirt of creamy Mechlin lace. The bodice and short puffed sleeves were also overlaid with lace, and it was belted with a matching blue velvet ribbon. She had got out the sapphire pendant Ralph had bought her in Paris, with its companion earrings, and her soft brown hair had been done in a cloud of curls. The overall impression was of exquisite fragility, and she smiled a little before going along to the nursery, as she had promised to show the children her gown.

Georgina's feelings were far different. She, too, had a new dress, of fine pink muslin trimmed with knots of darker pink ribbons. But her silhouette was anything but fragile, and as Lady Goring's maid applied the hot curling tongs to her pale blond hair, she frowned at her pudgy features in the dressing-table mirror. Everyone would laugh, Georgina thought. It was silly to fuss over her hair and to buy new gowns. She would be miserable at the ball, as always. She wished that she dared get out her box of chocolates in front of the maid. Dinner was late tonight, and she was hungry.

When Lady Goring, splendidly dressed in purple satin and amethysts, met her two charges in the drawing room some minutes later, her thoughts echoed theirs. She reveled in her daughter's beauty and despaired at Georgina's bulk. But she said merely, "We must hurry. What have you been doing, Anabel? You are late."

"The children kept me, admiring my lace." Anabel smiled. "Susan wants a gown exactly like this one for her birthday in September."

"And doubtless she will get it," answered her mother dryly. "I shudder to think what that child will be like at her come-out if she is demanding quite unsuitable dresses at the age of six."

"Susan will be a belle, of course. She is already pretty enough."

"And capricious enough," countered Lady Goring. "Come in to dinner."

* * *

The line of carriages beneath the glittering windows of the Rutland town house stretched far down the street as each halted briefly to deposit its elegantly dressed passengers, then moved on to make way for the next. The Goring party arrived in good time and, after greeting their hosts on the landing, made their way up to the half-filled ballroom. "Look at the flowers!" exclaimed Anabel at once.

"Very beautiful," responded her mother, surveying the great garlands of pink roses and greenery that festooned the walls. A trellis had been erected in one corner, and it looked remarkably natural.

"I have never seen so many roses in my life. Isn't it wonderful, Georgina?"

The younger girl nodded, but her eyes were on the other guests. Several were looking in their direction, probably talking of who they were and how dreadful she looked.

"I wish I had worn pink, as you did," added Anabel in an effort to cheer her.

Georgina merely looked disgusted.

"There is Jane Danvers," said Lady Goring. "Let us go and join her."

The room filled rapidly, and in a very short time the duchess gave the signal to begin the dancing. Anabel was asked at once, but Lady Goring had to summon a partner for Georgina, who accepted him with as little grace as he had showed at the command. When the first set ended, she escaped to the supper room, ignoring all frowns cast her way and hiding when Lady Goring came to search for her. Anabel, glowing from the country dance, was delighted when the orchestra struck up a waltz and more so when Sir Charles Norbury came up to claim her hand. She hadn't seen him arrive.

They moved onto the floor as the music began, and Norbury pulled her into a quick turn, making her very aware of the strength of his arm around her waist and the closeness of his body to hers. She felt small beside him, irresistibly guided by his whim. It was a new sensation, and uncertainty mixed with pleasure as they moved around the ballroom. Sir Charles remained an enigma to her. The men in her life had been very different—her father, a genial, uncomplicated creature extremely fond of his only daughter; Ralph, a bluff and hearty squire, pleased to have found such a wife; Christopher, a reliable, amusing friend. Norbury was none of these things, except perhaps amusing. In his polished looks, his assured, almost arrogant manner, and in the feeling of trembling excitement he engendered in her, he was unique in Anabel's life. She found him fascinating.

Norbury's thoughts were similar as they turned in the waltz and chatted. He had never encountered a woman precisely like Anabel. Most of those he knew had been schooled for years in the rituals of the *haut ton*, and the one or two countrywomen he had met had shown none of Anabel's easy understanding or quick wit. She was a curious mixture of naiveté and wisdom, and very pretty besides. He had had serious reservations about continuing his acquaintance with her when he discovered the existence of three tiresome children and their attendants. But Anabel's charm on their drive together had slowly disarmed his doubts. He enjoyed her company, he realized, more than that of any other female he could name, including his current inamorata. This was an odd circumstance, and one he wished to explore.

"Isn't that the lady you pointed out to me in the park?" asked Anabel then.

"Which?"

"There, in the puce satin. Did you not say that she has four daughters out at once?"

"I did indeed. The Marsden ensemble, each uglier than

the next. There they are, sitting in a row on that blue sofa."

"Where? Oh."

"Remarkably like a row of gargoyles on a cathedral porch, aren't they? Just as avaricious and terrifying."

"How can you?" But she couldn't help but laugh. There *was* something grotesque in the Marsden sisters' expressions.

"Easily. I have endured too many pretensions and too much fustian to be impressed by my fellowman any longer. Most of the people here, Lady Wyndham, are masterpieces of falsity and pettiness."

"Well, at least they are good at it, then."

"I beg your pardon?"

"If they are masterpieces, they must do it very well. That's something." She smiled up at him.

Sir Charles laughed. "Indeed, we certainly have the best of everything in London—the most single-minded greed, the greatest hypocrisy, the most refined cruelty."

"You are very severe."

"I have learned to be, watching this spectacle through the years." He gestured around them.

Anabel looked thoughtful. "I suppose you are very fond of Byron's poetry?"

"What?" Sir Charles was startled.

"Are you not? I said so only because that sounded very like some of it I have read." She didn't smile this time, but her eyes danced.

Her partner was speechless for several moments, then he laughed again. "You are astonishing," he said. "I don't believe anyone has ever spoken to me so."

"I suppose they are afraid of you."

"Afraid?"

"Knowing your low opinion of mankind. I am quite terrified myself. What will you say of me during the next set?"

He gazed down at her, shaking his head. "Nothing! I should not dare, for fear your wit would grow even sharper. Where, my dear Lady Wyndham, did you learn it?"

She shrugged, smiling again, and their eyes held as he spun her in a final turn to the conclusion of the music. Bowing over her hand, he said, "I believe they have shortened the length of the sets tonight. I never knew one to go so fast. Will you honor me again later?"

"Perhaps. If you ask me."

"You sound as if you do not think I will."

"I have been hearing a great deal about your reputation, Sir Charles. It seems that a woman mustn't set her heart on your promises."

"Ah. That depends on the woman." Another acquaintance had come up to ask Anabel for the set just forming, and Norbury stepped back. "I will see you later."

Anabel merely smiled, moving off on her new partner's arm. Norbury, watching her go, was surprised by the strength of emotion she had aroused in him in one short dance. She really was extraordinary.

From the doorway, another pair of eyes also followed her. Christopher Hanford had arrived in time to see Anabel dancing with Norbury, and apparently enjoying herself very much, and to observe their parting. It made him frown.

"That must be Anabel," murmured his sister. "She is very pretty, but what is she doing with Norbury? He is . . ." Christopher's frown had deepened at the name, and Amelia saw it. "Oh. I begin to understand. But, my word, Christopher—Norbury! A new coat is one thing; rivaling a noted Corinthian is quite another."

"No doubt," he said between clenched jaws.

His sister looked sidelong at him, then out over the ballroom. "Well, you cannot dance with her now. Come, I will present you to some of my friends."

She did so, including a number of the season's most charming debutantes. Hanford planned to flirt mildly with any who would respond, to see what Anabel made of that. But he found the girls very tiresome, and even before the set had ended, he was bored and irritated.

He looked around the room, his eyes lingering on Anabel before passing on. Lady Goring was surrounded by a group of her friends; he would greet her later. The few others he knew were dancing. His gaze came to the archway leading into the supper room, moved on, paused, and returned, recognizing a solid figure half visible there. "I am going to speak to someone, Amelia," he said.

"Who?"

"Anabel's cousin, Miss Goring. She is over there."

"That very *large* girl? But, Christopher, you mustn't be seen with a creature like that. Everyone will think you—"

"I may have put on the clothes of a popinjay, Amelia, but I refuse to take on their manner as well. Miss Goring is an intelligent girl, unlike those you have presented to me, and she is obviously having a very unpleasant time. It is simple kindness to speak to her."

Amelia acknowledged the truth of this with a sigh. Her brother would never change, and what was more, she was not sure she wanted him to.

Christopher grinned. "She is extremely fond of novels, Amelia. I imagine you have a great deal in common."

"I shall ask her to tea," replied his sister firmly. "But, Christopher . . . are you going to *dance* with her?"

He hadn't thought of it, but her tone made him rebellious. "Why, yes."

Georgina had disappeared when he turned to walk across the floor, but he found her inside the supper room, holding an ample plate of delicacies from the buffet and watching the entrance uneasily. When she saw him, she looked surprised, then cautiously pleased.

"Good evening, Miss Goring," he said. "I thought I saw you come this way."

Georgina's smile faded, and she lowered the plate a little while keeping a firm grip on it.

"Would you do me the honor of dancing this next set?" he continued.

The girl's mouth dropped open a little, and she stared at him.

"You do remember me? Christopher Hanford? I dined at Lady Goring's last week." Her stupefaction made him wonder if he had misjudged her intelligence.

"Yes. Yes, of course." Georgina was overcome. No gentleman had ever voluntarily asked her to dance in her life.

"Shall we?" He offered his arm.

Thrusting the plate aside without even looking at the table, Georgina took it, and they walked into the ballroom together. A country dance was just forming.

"Thank God it is not a quadrille," said Hanford. "I should quite disgrace you if it were."

"The steps are so complicated," agreed Georgina shyly. "I have never learned them properly."

Hanford smiled down at her as they took their places, and Georgina's heart turned over. A whole new world seemed to open out before her.

Conversation was difficult as they moved through the figures, and Hanford simply maintained his pleasant smile. Georgina smiled tremulously back throughout. He let his gaze wander about the room, discovering Anabel dancing on the other side and Amelia not far away. He would approach Anabel for the next waltz, he decided.

But Norbury was before him, and led Anabel onto the floor. A wave of anger so strong it made his hands clench sent Hanford to the prettiest deb his sister had presented to him. He secured her company for the waltz and concentrated all his faculties on amusing her, keeping the girl laughing throughout the set and the supper interval, which followed. He did not look at Anabel or at anyone else, distrusting his control if he had to watch her with Norbury. Thus, he saw neither her surprised glances nor Georgina Goring's woebegone expression.

When the dancing began again, he solicited another of the season's belles and then another. He ignored the Goring party and scarcely spoke to his sister, single-mindedly bent on showing Anabel that he, too, was attractive to the *haut ton*.

He succeeded very well. When he cared to exert it, Christopher Hanford had a quiet charm and humorous warmth that few women could resist. One girl after another came away from a dance thinking he was well worth cultivating, and determined to tell her mother to invite him at the first opportunity.

Anabel was also dancing during this time, but her eyes often strayed from her partner to follow Hanford. Sir Charles had left the ball for another gathering after supper, begging her pardon for the prior engagement, and as she had noticed Christopher's arrival some time before, she did not really mind. She was eager to talk with him and compare impressions of London. Too, he was looking more elegant than she had ever seen him, and she longed to tell him so and rally him about the change. She had consulted her mother about procuring invitations for Christopher, since he had decided to stay in town, and was prepared to surprise him with a number of them. She could not understand why he did not approach her. At first she had been merely puzzled, but as the ball continued and he devoted himself to one lovely eighteen-year-old after another, her bewilderment shifted to hurt, then anger.

The last dance of the evening was a waltz. Hanford, who had been carefully calculating his movements, joined Anabel at precisely the proper time to secure her hand for it. They walked onto the floor in silence, her chin high, and swung smoothly into step together. They had danced with each other many times, at private balls at home and at country assemblies, and they moved in perfect harmony. But Anabel's expression remained sulky, and Christopher, still angry at her for giving Norbury two waltzes, did not try to alter it.

"You have a new haircut," she said at last.

"Yes. My sister has taken me in hand."

"Your . . . oh, of course. I had forgotten she lives in London." Anabel felt an irrational chagrin. Christopher's sister would shepherd him through the intricacies of the season. He would need none of her feeble help.

"I must present you to her."

"That would be pleasant."

They had never been so carefully polite to each other before, and both felt and regretted the change. Abruptly Hanford relented. "You may tell me I look ridiculous if you like. I certainly feel it in these borrowed plumes."

"But you don't." Anabel looked squarely at him for the first time since his approach. "You look wonderful, Christopher. Very handsome indeed. As many would agree, from what I have seen tonight."

So she had noticed his dancing, he thought, his spirit lightening a little.

"I suppose your sister is gratified that you are ready to settle on a wife?"

"Oh, yes. She pushed all the debs on me."

"It is lucky you have such a zealous sponsor." Anabel's tone was sour, though she didn't hear it herself. Hanford smiled. "It was prodigious kind of you to include Georgina among your partners."

At this evidence that she had followed his progress closely, Hanford was even further cheered. "Miss Goring is an amiable girl."

It really *had* been kind, Anabel thought. Christopher remained the generous, selfless man he had always been. He deserved a flawless wife. Anabel, acknowledging this, wondered why she could not be happy about the prospect.

"Have you enjoyed the ball?" he asked.

"Oh, yes. It is much more grand than any I had seen before."

"Indeed. I suppose we shall both be surprised by a number of things in London before we return home again."

Anabel frowned up at him, trying to interpret this remark, but he whirled her suddenly around and forced her to turn her attention to her feet.

Chapter Six

Anabel woke the following morning conscious of a feeling of lassitude. Her memories of the ball were less exhilarating than she had expected. A pall seemed to hang over them. And as she washed and dressed and walked downstairs to breakfast, she felt tired and slightly headachy. What was wrong with her? she wondered. Surely any woman should be satisfied with a night like the last. She had danced every dance and been complimented on her looks several times. She had had the success of a young girl rather than the sedate entertainment of a widow, and she had enjoyed it very much. Never in her life had she been the focus of such varied and favorable attentions. Yet now she felt restless and irritable for no cause. It was extremely odd.

Her mother was already seated in the breakfast room with her morning letters and a boiled egg. As Anabel slipped into her chair Lady Goring looked up and said, "Your cousin Amory is very pleased with Vienna. And they will have a fourth child in the spring."

Anabel nodded, not deeply interested in this news of

her diplomatic cousin today. She poured herself a cup of tea and drank half of it quickly.

Lady Goring had opened another letter. "Julia Richards is a grandmother again," she said. "That must be the sixth . . . no, the seventh time. They are certainly a prolific family."

Anabel remained silent.

"Are you all right, dear? You look rather tired."

"I am, a little. I suppose I am not accustomed to late nights."

"You should have slept this morning. Your eyes are quite heavy."

"I'll be fine." A servant had brought hot toast, and Anabel took some and began to eat.

Lady Goring read her mail. The ticking of the clock on the mantelpiece was the only sound in the room for some time. Finally she put down the last envelope and refilled her teacup. "I wonder where Georgina . . . oh, there you are, dear. Did you sleep well?"

Georgina Goring, who had just entered the room, nodded as if abstracted. She was carrying a flat silver-paper box and a reticule clutched to her chest. Instead of going to her chair, she walked directly up to Lady Goring. "I want to give you these," she said breathlessly.

"What are they, dear?"

"Chocolates," she replied, putting the box down quickly, as if afraid she might not be able to do it. "And this is the pocket money my father gave me." She placed the reticule beside the box. "I want you to keep it for me, to use when we are shopping or . . . or something."

Lady Goring looked puzzled. "But, Georgina, you can manage your own allowance. I—"

"If you have it, I can't buy more chocolates," gasped the girl. She was finding the conversation very difficult, but she was determined to carry through.

"Can't . . ." Lady Goring's puzzled frown slowly shifted to surprise, then to amazed delight. "My dear Georgina, do you mean that you are taking my advice at last? How splendid! You will be very glad in the end, I promise you."

"Yes." Georgina did not sound very certain. She turned and started to leave the room.

"Where are you going?"

"To my room. I shall be upstairs if you want me."

"But you haven't had any breakfast. Sit down and let me ring for fresh tea."

Georgina gazed longingly at the table, with its toast racks and pots of jam, then at the sideboard, where chafing dishes held eggs and bacon, and a cold ham beckoned enticingly. She swallowed, her face anguished, then shook her head. "I . . . I'm not hungry."

"Not . . . Nonsense, of course you are hungry. It is very wise of you to give up sweets, Georgina, but you cannot stop eating altogether. Come and have a little. That is all you need do, you know, simply eat a little at each meal rather than . . ." Lady Goring let the sentence trail off, not wanting in any way to mar this miracle.

"That is harder than having nothing," wailed Georgina.

"Nonsense," replied her hostess again. "Come, sit down."

Slowly she did so. Anabel, who had been watching this exchange with some amusement, greeted her. Lady Goring beamed as she hurried to make up a frugal plate for her niece. Grimacing, Georgina began to eat.

Anabel could not resist probing a little for the cause of this change. "Did you enjoy the ball last night, Georgina?" she asked.

The girl seemed to find the question difficult. Finally she said, "Yes," in a tone that implied the negative as well.

"I saw you dancing with Mr. Hanford. I thought he looked very well in his new evening clothes."

Georgina's gray eyes abruptly shone. "Mr. Hanford is the most *wonderful* gentleman I have ever met!"

Lady Goring glanced meaningfully at her daughter, conveying a mutual understanding of Georgina's motives while hiding her own curiosity as to how Anabel would take this schoolgirl crush. She was certain of Christopher Hanford's feelings, but she was by no means privy to Anabel's.

Anabel was struggling with a violent, unreasoning annoyance. It was just like Christopher to encourage such a ridiculous passion, without being the least aware of doing so, of course. He was so kind to everyone. But he should realize that here in town things were quite different. Girls were not the daughters of old friends who could correctly interpret his behavior for their offspring. And the season naturally raised certain expectations. Its most exclusive assembly was known as the "marriage mart," after all. He was liable to find himself in a very awkward situation. Perhaps she should speak to him.

It was then that she remembered Christopher was in town to find a wife, and last night he had danced with every pretty ninnyhammer at the ball. He didn't require her advice. Far from it! But perhaps Georgina did. Looking across at her, Anabel frowned a little. Georgina had not begun eating again; she was gazing at the wall with a rapt expression. "He is certainly very kind," said Anabel. "I have rarely known a man so mindful of others' feelings."

"Oh, yes," agreed Georgina.

"Indeed, it is so marked that it is sometimes misinterpreted." Anabel, her attention focused on Georgina, did not see her mother's satisfaction at this remark. "On several occasions I have seen people make more of it than he meant."

The girl nodded. "I can see how that would happen. One must go beyond trivialities and discover true motives." She contemplated this a moment. "He danced with all those girls last night because they were pretty and amusing," she went on. "He thinks I am intelligent, however. And if I were also pretty . . ." She pushed away her plate and stood up. "I think I will go walking in the park this morning, aunt."

Lady Goring, who had been suppressing a smile, blinked. She had repeatedly urged Georgina to take exercise. "Splendid, my dear. Take your maid with you."

Nodding, the girl went out.

"Well!" said her aunt, gazing at Anabel expectantly. "What do you think of that."

Anabel also rose. Georgina's reasoning had shaken her. Christopher had called her intelligent, and if the girl's looks did improve under her new regimen, might he not possibly find the wife he desired in her? "Oh, it is all ridiculous!" she snapped, refusing to think about the implications of her feelings.

Lady Goring's eyes danced. "Well, I don't care why it is happening. I am only glad that Georgina has decided to do as I asked. I had nearly given up in despair." Savoring Anabel's mulish expression, she added, "Georgina will be a very pretty girl indeed if she slims, don't you think?"

"Doubtless." Anabel's tone was curt. "I shall be in my room if you want me, Mama." She swept out, leaving Lady Goring free to allow her pleased smile to spread across her face.

Striding quickly up the stairs, Anabel was oblivious to everything but her own ill temper. Everyone was being so stupid. Why couldn't Christopher behave as he always had? It was not that she begrudged him a season in London, she told herself, but he was almost certain to fall into a scrape. She was only thinking of him.

Immersed in her excuses, Anabel did not notice two small faces peering through the stair rails on the top landing.

She moved off below them toward her bedchamber, frowning, and they watched her go.

"Mama looks angry," said Susan in a low voice. "Isn't she coming up to see us before lessons? She always did at home."

"I don't know," answered Nicholas. "I suppose not."

"Is Uncle Christopher taking us to the play today? He promised he would."

Her brother sighed. This was not the first time, nor the twentieth, that Susan had asked this question. "He did not set a day. I'm sure he will do so when he has the time."

Susan stood, gripping the rails with her fists. "I hate it here!"

Nick nodded heavily. "Come along to the schoolroom. We must find William and have a council."

William was already there, sitting at the battered schoolroom table and scowling at an open book. He looked up when they came in. "I can't do this, Nick," he said. "Each time I work it out, I get a different answer. You must help me again."

"In a moment," replied his brother absently. "Just now we must decide something."

"What?" The older male Wyndham turned in his chair.

The others joined him at the ancient table. The schoolroom was a large, wide-windowed chamber near the top of the house, filled with castoff furniture from downstairs and the discarded toys and books of generations of Gorings. It was a comfortable, unpretentious place, but it was not their schoolroom and their mother was seldom in it, so the Wyndhams disliked it.

"We must make up our minds what we are going to do," declared Nicholas, putting his elbows on the tabletop and his chin in his hand.

"Are you still thinking of that?" William was resigned.

"I want to go home!" insisted Susan, her green eyes

glinting and her red hair brilliant in the shaft of sunlight from the window.

"I know, Susan, but we cannot," explained her elder brother.

"We might," objected Nicholas, "if we could just think of a plan."

"A plan," scoffed William.

"Try!" Nick's plea was so intense that all three frowned in thought, Susan's small face screwed up comically.

"You could pretend to be ill," William said to Nicholas then.

Nick, who had been considered sickly as a very small boy and strongly resented reminders of his weakness, answered, "Or you could fall into a truly dreadful scrape."

William scowled. He was prone to scrapes, often the result of his slower wits in carrying out one of his brother's plans. Susan looked interested.

"Or Susan could throw a particularly nasty temper tantrum," added Nick. "But I do not think any of those things would serve. Mama might simply send us home and remain here herself."

This prospect was so awful that they gazed at one another solemnly for a long moment. Then Susan jumped as if kicked. "Oh!"

"What?" said her brothers simultaneously.

She pointed toward the windows. Outside, on the narrow ledge, stalked Daisy, his bulk seeming much too wide for his perch. He was not looking at them but rather at a hapless sparrow twittering a few feet ahead.

"She'll fall!" shrieked Susan, leaping up and running to the window. "And if anyone sees her outside my room, she will be sent away. William! Nicholas! Do something!" Her screams frightened the bird, which flew away.

Daisy paused, disgusted, his eyes turning to glare at his

small mistress. He seemed quite comfortable on the window ledge.

"Don't be frightened, Daisy," said Susan. "We will get you down." She whirled to gaze at her brothers.

They rose reluctantly, particularly Nicholas. William carried his chair over to the window and climbed onto it to reach the catch. Then he threw up the sash and reached for the cat. Daisy backed away with a hiss.

"Daisy, come here!" commanded Susan. She started to scramble up beside William. The chair wobbled.

"Look out!" Nick cried.

With a shout from William, the chair toppled backward, flinging him heavily to the floor, with Susan kicking and protesting on top of him. Nick ran to see if they were all right. As he bent to help them up Daisy stuck his nose across the windowsill, took in the situation, and leaped solidly onto Nick's bent back, claws fully extended. They dug through the boy's coat and shirt to his skin and jerked him upright with a howl. Daisy jumped to the floor and ran under a convenient bookshelf.

"Devil take that cat!" cried Nick, with great satisfaction in at last having an opportunity to use an expression picked up from a stableboy. He snatched up the book William had been using and looked for Daisy, but the cat was well beyond his reach by this time.

"Nick!" screamed Susan. He put down the book.

William was on his feet, brushing the dust from his coat and looking intensely annoyed. "Of all the stupid—"

"I have it!" cried Nicholas. "It came to me just now." He noticed the others' blank stares with impatience. "The plan."

William pressed an elbow and winced. "Oh, no."

"It's a good one. Listen, what do we dislike most about London?"

"No fields. We hardly ever get out," responded William.

"Too many people telling us what to do," said Susan at the same time.

"Yes, yes. But that is not what we hate *most*." Nicholas paused for effect.

"Mama is always occupied or out," supplied Susan.

Her brother frowned at this anticipation of his words but nodded. "We were accustomed to seeing her every day, for hours. Now we never do. And she is always thinking of something else."

"We know *that*," said William.

"Well, let us do the same to her. Then she will see how unpleasant it is here."

"What do you mean?" They frowned at him.

"We must be too busy to see *her*. We must pretend that we have no time for visits and that we are interested in other things."

"But we are not!" exclaimed Susan. "There is nothing to be interested in here." She indicated the room with disgust.

"I know, Susan, but if we act as if there is, Mama will miss us just as we miss her, and she will take us home again, where we can all be comfortable."

"She will?"

William looked doubtful. "I don't know, Nicky. This sounds like one of your harebrained schemes. Mama hardly notices what we do lately. She won't care."

"She doesn't notice because we are just as we always were. If we changed, she would wonder soon enough. I only worry that Susan will forget and spoil the whole plan."

"I can do anything you can do," protested his sister at once. But she looked confused. "What am I to do?"

"Just pretend you do not care whether Mama comes to us or not, and that you have a great many more interesting things to do when she does."

Susan's full lower lip protruded. "That will be very hard."

"It will, Nick," agreed William. "I don't know if *I* can do it. Without Mama . . ."

"We shall have each other," insisted Nicholas. "And we must always remember that playing our parts will get us home again and make things as they used to be." He looked from one to the other. "Will you try?"

William and Susan had learned to trust Nick's intelligence. After a moment they nodded.

"Good, here is what we must—"

The door opened, and a tall, spare young woman entered. "You are all here. Splendid. We can begin at once."

Nicholas closed his mouth, and the three children shuffled into their chairs around the table. In the country their mother had supervised their lessons each morning, but here in London Lady Goring had insisted on a governess. Miss Tate was neither unkind nor unamusing, but she was still a stranger, and her substitution for Lady Wyndham made the children slow to warm to her. They did their lessons and generally obeyed her commands but did not offer confidences or affection as yet.

As they fetched books and pencils Nicholas signaled the others with jerks of his head and grimaces that they would finish their conference after studies. He was extremely pleased with himself, certain that his idea would work within a fortnight. As always, the exercise of his intelligence exhilarated him, and he even managed to slip William the answer to the problem that had been plaguing him without Miss Tate seeing.

Chapter Seven

The first few weeks of the season passed quickly. Neither Anabel nor Christopher had ever experienced such a whirl of social activity, and Georgina was almost dazed by the constant round. To Lady Goring's amazement and gratification, her niece maintained her resolve to avoid chocolates and other sweets, and the effects soon became apparent. Georgina's face looked more slender within just a few days, and her figure slowly followed suit. The image that emerged was quite engaging, and Lady Goring was certain that she would be very pretty indeed if she continued. Georgina herself, astonished at the reflection her mirror showed her, became even more Spartan in her self-discipline and often had to be urged to eat.

Anabel watched the process with a mixture of amused encouragement and chagrin, for though she was happy that Georgina should feel more comfortable in town, she always felt an irrational annoyance when she saw the girl with Christopher. Her adoration was so patent, and yet he did nothing to discourage it. Anabel felt someone ought to speak to him, but for some reason she hesitated to do so herself.

For one thing, she was too busy. They went out nearly every night, and as the days passed, Anabel became more certain of seeing Sir Charles Norbury at each event they attended. At first she had met him only intermittently, and she heard that he was known for ignoring invitations he judged boring. His presence at a party was considered a great coup. But as time went on, he turned up at more and more of the gatherings and practically devoted himself to her. People began to gossip about it, and Anabel knew she should withdraw, but Norbury continued to fascinate her. His polished manners, sardonic opinions of the world of fashion, and aura of barely controlled passions attracted her despite whatever firm resolves she made. When he approached her, she forgot the staring crowds in the heady new game of flirtation. And when some brief flash in Norbury's pale green eyes suggested that it was more than a game, Anabel felt a tremor of excitement and half-apprehensive anticipation.

Watching this spectacle, Christopher Hanford grew progressively more dour, though it was obvious only to those most interested in the outcome. He flirted with the debs, danced, and drank champagne among the *haut ton*, but his gaze was most often fixed on the woman he was *not* partnering, and he moved like an automaton through society's rituals, scarcely aware of what he said or did. He was losing Anabel, he knew, and nothing else mattered to him. His sister rarely looked at him without a frown now, and Lady Goring was filled with annoyance and concern for both him and her daughter. Yet nothing either said appeared to make a particle of difference.

In this charged atmosphere the children's scheme fell rather flat. They exerted themselves mightily to carry out Nicholas' orders, but their mother hardly seemed to notice the withdrawal. Once or twice, when she visited them in the nursery, she wondered that they did not greet her more enthusiastically, but Anabel's mind was too occupied with her own situation to concentrate on anything else. Nicholas was much downcast by the failure, and Susan and William were indignant.

By the beginning of Georgina's second month in London, Lady Goring was feeling so pleased with her that she determined to give a ball for her charge. There had been no such entertainment at the Goring house for nearly a year, and she felt in the mood to give one. If she could have discovered some excuse for *not* asking Sir Charles Norbury, she would have been perfectly content.

She could not, however, and when the gilt-edged invitation cards went out, one was addressed to him. They received a flattering number of acceptances, considering the rather impromptu nature of the ball, and Lady Goring threw herself into the preparations, with occasional help from Georgina. She was so busy that she scarcely noticed Anabel's lack of participation or her frequent absences during the day. And, indeed, Anabel's mind was in such turmoil that she would not have been of much use. Norbury's attentions had become so marked, so unmistakable, that she knew she could expect a declaration soon. Even the gossips had altered their tone. Norbury was notorious for his intense, and short-lived, flirtations, and he customarily conducted them with willing young matrons, who could not threaten him with marriage. At first Anabel's widowhood had seemed to put her in the same class, but when Norbury's campaign continued and even intensified, the *ton* began to look more closely. What they saw suggested to more than one gossip that Sir Charles' famous immunity to serious attachments had at last given way. This was ten times more interesting than his flirtations, and the talk redoubled, with gentlemen placing bets at their clubs on the timing of the announcement in the *Morning Post*.

Anabel found this public scrutiny of her private affairs highly unsettling. She began to feel reluctant to enter crowded drawing rooms, and the knowledge that she could expect an offer, without any certainty as to when, strung her nerves too tight. Worst of all, she was not completely sure how she felt about Norbury. It seemed very soon to make a decision, though she knew many women made such a choice after even shorter acquaintance. Nonetheless, she felt hurried. There seemed too many elements to consider; they all rose up to badger and confuse her. When she was with Sir Charles, the thrill of his presence dispelled her doubts, but when he was gone, she again wondered. It was a new experience; Anabel had accepted Ralph Wyndham on her parents' recommendation, never thinking of refusing. She had had no practice in the games of courtship.

On the night of the ball, Lady Goring, Anabel, and Georgina met early in the drawing room to receive a few dinner guests before the main entertainment. They had had new dresses made up for the occasion, and each in her own way looked splendid.

Lady Goring had chosen an emerald silk whose brilliance and sheen were merely enhanced by the very simple cut. She wore emeralds and diamonds, and had fastened a spray of them in her hair.

Anabel wore a warm peach satin embroidered around the hem and sleeve with ivory blossoms. Ivory ribbons fluttered at the high waist, and one of the cameos her grandmother had brought back from Paris years ago was fastened close about her throat. She looked cool and untouchable as a Dresden shepherdess, but inside she was seething with expectation and uncertainty.

Georgina's appearance was the most remarkable. In the

weeks since her revelation she had shed a surprising amount of her bulk. She was still far from sylphlike, but the fashion of the day was charitable toward a slight thickening of the waist and hip. In a gown of floating white muslin, with sleeves cut to the elbow and a generous flounce about the hem, she made a very creditable show. And her face was by now almost beautiful. As its fullness declined, the finely sculpted bones became evident, and her thickly lashed gray eyes seemed larger and more expressive. Tonight a becoming color stained her cheeks, and her pale hair had been dressed by Lady Goring's maid into a helmet of curls. Georgina was trembling with excitement.

"Well," said Lady Goring, sinking onto the sofa. "I believe we are actually ready at last. I cannot think of a single thing left to do. If you had asked me last week, I would have vowed this moment would never come!"

"The ballroom is wonderful," breathed Georgina.

"It does look well, doesn't it?" answered her aunt complacently. "I must say, I think it was a good idea to use the ivy. Don't you, Anabel?"

Her daughter started. "What? I beg your pardon, Mama?"

Lady Goring frowned at her, hesitated, then shook her head. She was beginning to think that her husband had been right when he married Anabel off without a come-out.

There were sounds of arrival in the front hall below, and in a moment a footman was announcing Christopher Hanford and his sister and brother-in-law. Lady Goring greeted them warmly, Georgina with tremulous smiles and Anabel abstractedly. Hanford frowned and turned to the younger girl. "You are looking very pretty tonight, Georgina," he said.

She swallowed, trying to dislodge the lump in her throat. "Th-thank you."

"I hope you are saving a dance for me." He was gazing

sidelong at Anabel as he spoke; she didn't seem aware of anyone.

"Oh, yes!"

The fervency of her answer transfixed him. Surveying Georgina more closely, Hanford made a discovery. The girl was deep in the throes of calf love, and he himself was the object! He almost groaned aloud. He wanted to concentrate all his faculties on Anabel, and here was this schoolgirl with worship shining in her eyes. It wasn't fair.

Meeting her unwavering gaze again, he sighed, then smiled. Calf love was one of the most dreadful experiences in life, as he well remembered. He had to do what he could to ease her through and out of it.

More dinner guests were ushered in, and after a few minutes they went in to dinner. Norbury had not been included in this party—Lady Goring had been determined on that, at least, and Anabel had not objected. There were two old friends of hers, carefully chosen parents of offspring about Georgina's age, and their sons and daughters. Georgina was seated between two of the former, to ensure her partners for some of the dances, and Anabel was cunningly placed beside Hanford. Georgina at first resented this exile, but when the young men seemed inclined to admire her, she unbent and, to her own astonishment, found things to say that made them both laugh.

"We haven't talked much recently," said Hanford over the first course. "It seems odd, after the way we used to do so in the country." He was ready to use whatever weapons he could now—to give up flirting, to return to his old coats—if that would win Anabel away from the hated Norbury.

"Yes," she agreed. "It is very different here, of course."

"Very. How are the children? They seemed a trifle out of sorts when I saw them last week."

"When did you see them? They didn't mention it to

me." Anabel was astonished. The children always described their outings to her in great detail.

"We went riding. I thought they would like it, as they are accustomed to get out at home. We found a fine pony for Susan at the livery."

"How kind of you." Anabel's reply was a bit faint. She was wondering why she had not thought of providing the children with mounts. They adored riding. And why had they not told her? Suddenly anxious, she frowned down at her plate.

Hanford saw it with pleasure. Perhaps he could still reach her. "I promised we should go again on Friday. Will you come with us?"

She nodded. "I should like to."

"Good." He left the matter there, satisfied that the hints he had thrown out would stay with her, and the conversation drifted to more general topics.

They didn't linger at table. By nine the party had moved to the ballroom, and Lady Goring was greeting the first new arrivals under the archway. The room soon filled, and Georgina was called upon to play the part she had been dreading—opening the dancing with a young man presented to her by Lady Goring. She was quaking when the music struck up, but as they moved through the steps and her partner made it clear that he did not feel the task a penance, she felt better. By the end of the set she was even smiling at him and talking in a voice that was nearly normal.

Anabel had not joined the first set. Still vaguely worried, she had slipped upstairs to look at the children. She had bade them good night earlier, after showing them her ball gown, but she needed to see them again to reassure herself of their well-being after Hanford's surprising revelations. Susan was fast asleep, curled in a tight ball and clutching a tattered rag doll that she claimed only at night. She looked angelic, and Anabel smiled at the deceptiveness of sleep as she tucked the blanket closer around her neck. No one would guess her daughter's strong will from this picture. The boys were in bed but not yet quite asleep. They blinked up at her candle when she came in and asked what was wrong. "Nothing. I just came up to say good night." She bent to kiss each of them, her throat tightening at their hugs and the fresh child smell of their skin. She missed them, she suddenly realized. They had seen much more of one another at home. "I am going riding with you and Uncle Christopher on Friday," she whispered.

"You are!" They bounced up, eyes shining.

"Yes. But you must lie down now. It is late."

It took her a while to get them settled and, indeed, she lingered a little, feeling very happy. But at last they were quiet, falling into sleep, and she took up her candlestick and slipped out again. The music from the ballroom filtered up the stairs, and she moved down them slowly, her blue eyes soft with memory.

"There you are," said someone from the hall below. "They said you had gone upstairs."

She looked down to find Sir Charles Norbury gazing up at her. A tingling shock ran through her body, and the candle trembled a little, dripping wax.

"You have missed the first waltz," he added, meeting her at the bottom of the staircase and taking the candlestick from her hand. He snuffed the flame between forefinger and thumb and set it aside. "And I came early especially to engage you for it."

"I wanted to look in on the children." As always, his presence overwhelmed her. He seemed to tower over her, yet his pale green eyes felt close and compelling. She found it hard to breathe.

"It is a country dance now, unfortunately. Mayn't we wait outside here for the next and hope?" He smiled and reached for her hand to lead her across to a small empty anteroom.

Anabel knew she should say no, but her voice seemed to have died, and she went with him silently and allowed him to escort her to a sofa and sit beside her, his arm thrown along its back.

"You look exquisite tonight," he said softly. "The loveliest woman at the ball."

This outrageous compliment revived her. "What a plumper. There are dozens of prettier ones."

"No."

"Flatterer." She smiled, but when she met his eyes, they were very serious.

"No," he said again. "To me you are the most beautiful." He held her gaze for a moment, then slowly bent forward and took possession of her lips, his arm tightening around her shoulders.

Anabel's slight trembling increased, and her mind dissolved in confusion. She should pull away, part of it cried; this was terribly fast, and someone might come in at any moment. But another part urged her on, fascinated by Sir Charles' attractions and filled with curiosity.

His kiss was very expert, and nothing at all like her deceased husband's, Anabel's only standard of comparison. His lips seemed to draw all strength out of her, leaving her limp and pliant, yet she felt disconnected from the expected sensual pleasure. He knew how to draw response from her body, clearly, but her heart and mind remained in turmoil.

Norbury, on the contrary, was in the grip of feelings stronger than any he had ever experienced, and for him the kiss confirmed a decision. This was the woman he wanted. Never had his passions been suffused with such emotion. Beyond thinking, he moved his free hand to Anabel's knee and slid it upward caressingly, savoring the curve of her waist under the thin satin dress and cupping his fingers around her breast. She drew her breath in sharply.

A scuff of footsteps in the hall, followed by a scrap of conversation and a laugh, jerked Anabel upright. She pulled away from him only just in time to avoid being caught by two couples coming into the room. But it was obvious in the way that the newcomers stopped, smiled, and apologized that their appearance gave them away. Anabel rose and hurried from the room, Norbury behind her. Her cheeks were flaming, and she felt that she could not possibly face the crowd in the ballroom.

Sir Charles caught her arm and turned her to face him. "I beg your pardon. That was entirely my fault, and I apologize. I would not worry you or expose you to embarrassment for the world."

"It . . . it doesn't matter," replied Anabel, her voice a little choked.

"On the contrary. Lady Wyndham . . . Anabel, you must know that I have something to ask . . ." A laughing couple came out of the ballroom and stood nearby, the lady fanning herself and complaining of the heat. Norbury scowled. "We cannot talk here. If you . . ." Looking at her face, he realized that this was no time to suggest they withdraw. "May I call on you at eleven tomorrow morning?" he finished.

Anabel couldn't think of anything but escaping from prying eyes. "Yes, of course."

Sir Charles bowed his head, then offered his arm. "They are playing a waltz at last. We can slip in among the dancers without attracting undue notice."

Nodding, she took his arm. They moved to the archway, and Norbury guided her deftly among the circling couples. Even the ones nearest hardly glanced at them. Anabel sighed with relief and relaxed a little in his arms.

"All will be well," he murmured.

But all was not well for several people in the ballroom who had been on the watch for Anabel. Christopher Hanford, dancing with Georgina, was barely able to control the hot surge of rage at the sight, and his fist closed convulsively, nearly crushing the girl's hand. "What is the matter?" she exclaimed.

"Nothing, nothing." He had been trying his best to be at once kind and unencouraging to Georgina, but now he had no thought to spare for her. His face fell into hard lines, and he kept his eyes on Anabel.

Georgina, scanning his features anxiously, searched her meager experience for the proper words. This had been the most wonderful evening of her life. Several young men had asked her to dance without being prompted, and now she was in the arms of the gentleman she most admired. She had been approved to waltz by Almack's patronesses only tonight, and this was the first time she had tried that stimulating dance. Everything had been perfect until a moment ago. What should she say? She wanted very much to comfort Hanford, to both share and erase the trouble she saw in his face, but she didn't know how. Biting her lower lip, she followed his lead and worried.

The other two who had seen Anabel come in had moved toward each other soon after. Lady Goring and Amelia Lanforth had met recently, and despite the difference in their ages, they had discovered much in common. A series of meaningful looks at an evening party two nights before had assured them that they shared certain hopes for Anabel and Christopher. They had said nothing aloud, but tonight's developments dissolved their reserve.

"He is going to offer for her," said Amelia in a low voice when they had left a group of friends. "I can hardly believe it."

Lady Goring did not have to ask whom she meant. Her daughter's face when she returned to the ballroom, and Norbury's, had told her a great deal. "I wish I had never made her come to London," she repined.

"You think she'll accept him?" Amelia's eyes shifted to her brother. He was staring at Anabel in the most transparent way, she saw.

"I fear it, though I can't say for certain."

"Christopher will be so unhappy."

Lady Goring merely shook her head. "Norbury is a great catch, but not the sort of man I would want for my daughter."

"He seems to care for her," replied Amelia, trying to be comforting. When the other did not answer, she added, "I suppose there is nothing we can do?"

"I have tried talking to her, more than once. She won't listen."

"Ah." They watched the set end and the couples break apart. Hanford escorted Georgina to them and turned away without a word, almost stalking across the floor to Anabel. They watched him stop before her, speak, and then lead her away despite an involuntary restraining gesture from Norbury. Both men were frowning. Norbury stood alone for a moment, but he soon recognized that their exchange had drawn notice. He set his lips and walked out of the room.

Christopher, taking Anabel's hand as the music started again, was silently grim. She did not see it at first, still too wrapped up in her own concerns. But as the dance went on and he did not speak, she finally looked up, encountering an angry gaze. "What's wrong?"

"Wrong?"

She had never heard him use such a cold, angry tone. And she had never seen his face so haughty and withdrawn.

This was not her old reliable friend Christopher but some daunting, fashionable stranger. Had the whole world gone mad?

"Perhaps I am disappointed to see you become one of the *on-dits* of the town," he added between his teeth. "If you wish to make a fool of yourself in public, I cannot, of course . . ."

This was too much, after her embarrassing return to the ballroom. How could he imagine she had done it on purpose? "It is none of your affair what I do!" she snapped.

He had to wait a moment before answering. He was so angry that he was afraid he would shout. "Perhaps not," he managed finally, "though some would say that years of friendship gave me a claim. However, as you do not acknowledge that, and since you appear to have no respect for my opinions, I—"

"Please say no more!" Anabel's brain was whirling. In nearly ten years she and Christopher had had no such disagreements. She had always believed that they had wholly congenial tempers and ideas. And even if he disapproved of her conduct tonight, not realizing that it had been unintentional, she did not understand why he should attack her so viciously. Could he not see how it hurt her? Indeed, it hurt so much that she was having trouble keeping time to the dance. That strangers might think her imprudent had been upsetting; that Christopher should was somehow many times worse. It seemed to Anabel that everything in her life was going awry.

They finished the set in silence. Hanford's mouth was thin and unforgiving, and Anabel kept her perpetually tearing eyes on the floor. She was miserable, and had never been more grateful than when the music ended and she could retreat upstairs to the room set aside for the ladies.

Christopher left the ball without speaking to anyone. He couldn't bear any more talking, and his heart sank when he thought of the future. Anabel was slipping away from him, and he was helpless to do anything about it.

Chapter Eight

Sir Charles was exactly on time the following morning. Anabel received him in the library rather than the drawing room because her mother's reaction to the impending visit had been so carefully unemotional that Anabel decided it would be better if they did not meet. She had put on a white muslin gown delicately striped with a blue that matched her eyes and dressed her soft brown hair in curls, but she did not feel she looked her best. She had not slept well after the ball. Consciousness of the approaching decision and worry over Christopher and the children had kept her tossing on her pillow for hours.

Anabel had never endured such uncertainty. The large problems of life had always been settled by someone else. Her father had decreed her marriage, then Ralph had taken his place. When Ralph died, she had naturally turned to Christopher for help with the arrangements and all business matters. Anabel had run her house and cared for her children, but she had never really determined the course of her life. Now, with her mother noncommittal and Christopher incomprehensibly cold and withdrawn, she had to, and the knowledge made her uneasy.

Norbury looked splendid in a coat of olive-green super-fine and buff pantaloons. His Hessian boots gleamed as he followed the footman into the room, and his waistcoat was a model of fashion and propriety. As she held out her hand to him Anabel thought how handsome he was. He was the most impressive figure she had ever been intimate with.

"I hope you have recovered from last night," he said with a smile.

Her heart beat faster. "Yes." She didn't feel able to tell him she felt tired and heavy-eyed.

"Shall we sit down?"

"Oh. Of course." Moving to the sofa before the fireplace, she did so. Norbury sat close beside her.

"I can think of nothing else, so I will come directly to the point," he went on. His green eyes were very serious. "I believe you know what I wish to say to you. I have fallen in love with you and hope you will be my wife."

Anabel trembled a little. Though she had expected the question, still, to hear it was exciting. She looked up and met his steady gaze. The gossips had been eager to tell her of Norbury's past flirtations; her own mother had made it clear that he was a man of wide experience and impervious heart. He had examined scores of debutantes with a jaundiced eye and sampled the charms of a series of stunning older women, but he had never offered his hand. Anabel was by no means unaware of her unique position. His proposal would cause a sensation. She would be envied and honored for her conquest. It was terribly flattering to be the choice of such a man. His wealth and position were nothing to it.

And the man himself was an added inducement. As always in his presence, Anabel felt fascinated and attracted. Sir Charles radiated confidence. Something in the set of his head, the way he moved and looked at her, made her vibrate with an unidentifiable tension. The memory of his touch made her feel slightly faint. He overwhelmed her.

"You must say something, you know," he said.

The command made her look down again. What did she want? she wondered. She didn't really know. Her wants had always been supplied to her almost before they were formulated. She had wanted what she had been expected to desire and accepted others' giving of it. Her father, Ralph, Christopher, had seemed certain of what was right, and she had left matters to them. She was accustomed to that. Now, for the first time, she was being asked to choose for herself—and her choice did not have to be the safe one. Meeting Norbury's eyes again, and feeling that quivering thrill, she slowly nodded. "Yes."

He smiled and took her hand, letting out his breath. "You made me quite uneasy for a moment. I didn't realize how difficult it could be to wait for a word." He kissed her hand. "I shall do my utmost to be an exemplary husband, Anabel. As I am sure you have been told, my record is not a good one. But that is past. Having met you, I am yours alone."

Anabel said nothing. She was feeling confused. Having made her decision, she ought to be happy, she thought, but she felt only relief that it was over and she need worry no longer.

"Why so silent?" he teased, putting his arm along the sofa back around her shoulders. "You have not even assured me you return my flattering sentiments, you know."

Gazing at him, Anabel could see that his light tone masked sincerity. He wanted her to say she loved him. She opened her mouth to do so—she must or she would not have accepted him—and stopped. It suddenly seemed to her that she didn't know what the word meant. Or, more to the point, she didn't know in this case. She loved her mother and had loved her father; she adored her children. But for her husband she had always felt a kind of warm, ironic affection different from both of these feelings and very different from those Sir Charles elicited. If she had loved Ralph . . . but had she? Perhaps not; perhaps what she felt now was really love—this trembling excitement and uncertainty. "I . . . I do." She faltered, her voice sounding false in her own ears.

Norbury did not seem to hear it. He smiled and drew her closer. "I had begun to fear that this moment would never come, that I would never find a woman with whom I could spend my life. You are very precious to me, Anabel." Bending, he kissed her. Once again Anabel felt that melting sensation in all her bones. His practiced hands knew just how to move, and she felt as if she were being carried away by an irresistible tide. She was powerless, motiveless; all her senses swam.

It was some time before Norbury pulled away. His breathing had quickened, and his green eyes were clouded with desire. He held her away from him and laughed shakily. "Enough of that, I'm afraid. I can't answer for myself otherwise. You fill my veins with fire, Anabel."

She blushed a little, half flattered, half confused. No one had ever said such things to her before.

He took a deep breath and straightened. "When shall the wedding be? Soon."

"I . . ." She hadn't thought further than the proposal.

"Next month? There is no reason for us to wait."

"But I must tell my mother, my family."

He smiled. "That will hardly take a month. Let us set it for a month from today."

He was so eager that she found it hard to resist him. But she wasn't ready to go this far. "We can decide that later, can we not? There is so much to do."

Norbury frowned, then shrugged. "Very well. I'll send the announcement to the *Morning Post* today, and you can begin your vast preparations." He smiled again. "You must come down to Kent and meet my mother. She doesn't get to London now. She will be delighted. Shall I tell her next week?"

"I . . ." Anabel felt overwhelmed by all these sudden plans.

"We don't want to leave it too long."

"I suppose I can."

"Splendid. I'll write her today."

She made an effort to contribute something. "You must become better acquainted with my children also. Shall we go out together?"

Norbury's smile faded a bit. In his infatuation with Anabel, he had tried to forget that she was burdened with a family. He didn't want to think of her as another man's wife or as the mother of any but his children. "Of course."

She caught the change in his tone and looked up anxiously. "I'm sure you will love them when you know them."

"No doubt."

"When shall we go? Monday, perhaps?"

"I had thought of starting for Kent Monday."

"Oh. Well, before that, then." She frowned. "They are right here, after all. You needn't go anywhere."

Seeing her growing concern, he nodded. "I can be free for a while on Saturday morning."

It seemed a grudging acceptance, and Anabel's frown remained.

"Where would they like to go, do you think?" he added. "I know very little about children."

"They love the park. We could go walking."

He nearly grimaced, but her expression made him suppress it. There would be plenty of time to deal with the children later. "I will see what I can arrange."

She smiled, relieved, though he had set no time.

"And now I should go, I suppose." He rose. "We shall be very busy for the next few weeks."

She got up and walked with him to the library door. There he paused and pulled her into his arms again, molding the length of her body to his. Anabel put her arms around him, feeling the movement of hard muscle in his back. "I can scarcely wait so long," he murmured before bending to kiss her again.

Only his embrace held her upright as his hands caressed her shoulders and back. She was again swept away by a tide of intense sensation. Her brain whirled with it, and when he drew away again, she found it hard to breathe.

"I shall see you tonight," he said, smiling. "And the announcement will be published tomorrow." He went into the front hall, and she followed him shakily.

When he was gone, Anabel returned to the library for a few moments to regain her composure. She must go upstairs and tell her mother and the children, she knew, but not just yet. She wanted to explore her own feelings first. She should be happy, she thought, but she wasn't. She was breathless and confused, and wished she had someone to talk with about the events of the day. Her mother would be unsympathetic, and there was no other woman in London to whom she could turn. She thought suddenly of Christopher. How comforting it would be to ask his advice and receive his usual sane, sensible counsel. The thought of Christopher was like a rock in the swirling chaos of her emotions. He would know what was right. But as soon as she thought it, she shook her head. She couldn't go to him about this. Even had they been on their former easy footing, it wouldn't be proper. And now that Christopher was so changed, it was out of the question.

Abruptly Anabel felt terribly dispirited. Her life had been so simple once; now it seemed unmanageably complex.

And for the first time she had no one to turn to for help. This, naturally, led her thoughts to Sir Charles. He was the logical source of aid after this morning. But somehow she could not imagine going to him with her problems. He was not that sort of person. And he was too much a part of her uncertainty to understand or judge it.

Sighing, Anabel rose and started upstairs. She had to speak to her mother. The announcement would come out tomorrow, and she must be told well before then.

Lady Goring was sitting with Georgina in the drawing room, looking over some new dress patterns. But she looked up when Anabel came in, her expression concerned. "I have good news, Mama," said Anabel.

Her mother's face went rigid. "Yes, dear?"

"Sir Charles Norbury and I are going to be married."

Lady Goring nodded, as if taking an expected blow, and said, "I see. And are you very sure, Anabel, that this is what you want?"

Her own doubts receded before opposition. "Of course, Mama. I should not have accepted otherwise."

"Yes. Well, I wish you happy, dear." Lady Goring rose and embraced her daughter, smiling with an effort.

"Sir Charles Norbury?" put in Georgina, who had been sitting very still, eyes wide, since Anabel made her announcement. "How can you?"

"What do you mean?" asked Anabel, annoyed.

The girl blushed furiously. "I beg your pardon. I didn't realize I had spoken aloud."

"Sir Charles is a very charming man."

"Oh, yes. Of course. I mean, I hardly know him, and I am sure he is much kinder with *you*. I don't . . . that is, I never . . ." She paused, struggling to amend her slip. "He frightens me, that's all."

"Frightens you?" In her defensive anger, Anabel was contemptuous. "That's ridiculous!"

Georgina nodded humbly. "I daresay it is only because I am so unfamiliar with society. He just seems so grand and . . . *above* everyone. If I should have to speak to him, I should be terrified of receiving a dreadful setdown."

Lady Goring looked as if she agreed, but she said nothing.

"Nonsense," replied Anabel, with an uncomfortable feeling that there was something in what Georgina said. Charles did not particularly enjoy talking to her. "And you *will* speak to him. Often. He will be here a great deal now."

"Oh." Georgina looked apprehensive, then brightened. "But he will wish to be with you, of course."

Anabel's frown led her mother to intervene. "We must have him to dinner soon, to meet the whole family. Will you discover a good day, Anabel?"

"Yes."

"I suppose we must have your great-aunts. It is too bad your papa is so far off, Georgina."

The girl seemed doubtful about this, but she said nothing.

"I will be going to Kent to visit the Norburys next week," added Anabel.

"Ah. Old Lady Norbury is quite formidable, I understand." Lady Goring had been observing her daughter carefully, and her eyes were now brighter with cautious hope. Anabel did not show the bubbling happiness a love match usually engendered. Indeed, she looked positively petulant. Perhaps there was still a chance.

"I must go up and tell the children," was her daughter's only reply. As Anabel turned and left the room Lady Goring exchanged a glance with Georgina. Then she opened the pattern book once again.

On the stairs, Anabel felt immediate relief. Mama might really have more sympathy with her, she thought. One could not expect Georgina to understand anything, but Mama should try to enter into her feelings. She was no green girl attaching herself to a fortune hunter, after all.

Charles was eminently eligible, a great catch in fact. It would be very good to reach the nursery. Her children had been her greatest source of happiness and comfort for years now.

The young Wyndhams were at their lessons when Anabel came in. In the past her arrival would have been the excuse for immediate abandonment of books and a great flurry of welcome and exuberant embraces. Today, however, the boys merely looked up and said hello. Susan leaped from her low chair, then seemed to think of something and sat down again. The governess raised her eyebrows. She didn't approve of parents who interrupted the lesson period.

"Excuse me, Miss Tate," said Anabel, smiling apologetically. "I'm sorry to take time from schoolwork, but I have something rather important to discuss with the children."

The governess inclined her head and rose, leaving the nursery with a distinct air of disapproval. Anabel grinned conspiratorially at the children, but Nick and William were still bent over their books, and Susan quickly suppressed her impish response. Anabel felt disproportionately aggrieved. Did no one in her family care a rap for her feelings? What was wrong with the children? They had never been like this. Chagrin made her abrupt. "I have something to tell you, children," she said. "Some good news."

Susan looked eager. "We are going home?"

Anabel's annoyance increased. "No. I have told you over and over that we shall spend several months in London."

Susan, whose idea of the length of a month was hazy, pouted.

"I am going to be married," continued Anabel. "You will have a new papa."

All three of them stared at her, stunned.

Anabel moved uncomfortably under their gaze, feeling

she hadn't handled the revelation particularly well. "He is Sir Charles Norbury. You met him in the drawing room one day. Remember?"

There was another shocked silence, then Susan burst out, "I *hate* him!"

"Susan!"

"I do! And so does Daisy!"

"Nonsense. You have hardly spoken two words to him. You will like him very well when you know him better."

Susan's small mouth set in an obstinate line. "Shan't!"

Exasperated, Anabel turned to her sons. "Have you nothing to say?"

Nicholas still looked stunned, but William, conscious of his responsibilities as the oldest, made an effort to pull himself together. "We . . . we wish you very happy, Mama."

"You will be happy, too." Anabel felt goaded. "You have always wished for someone to take you hunting and teach you to shoot."

"Uncle Christopher is going to do that!" blurted Nick, then flushed. "I mean, he *was*."

Anabel nearly snapped back at him, but she restrained herself. This was wholly unexpected news to the children, she realized, and they could hardly be blamed for their reaction. When they had had time to take it in, they would no doubt feel better about the change. Though some part of her remained unconvinced by this argument, she said, "We shall be very happy together. You will see. Sir Charles is coming to dinner very soon, and you will all be allowed to dine downstairs to meet him. He is very charming." Nagging doubt tried to surface again, and she suppressed it.

"He's a blighter," answered Susan, using a word whose power she knew by Nurse's horror when she had first uttered it.

But Anabel simply laughed. "Mind your tongue, Susan.

Where did you hear such an expression?" Looking from one to another pair of wide, reproachful eyes, she hesitated. "Everything will be all right. You'll see."

They continued to gaze at her.

"We shall be a whole family again," added Anabel, less strongly. And when their expressions did not change, she was overcome by a kind of cowardice. "I must let you get back to your lessons. We are going riding tomorrow, don't forget." With a falsely bright smile, she left them.

When the door had closed, there was a short pause, then William burst out, "This is all your fault, Nick!"

"Mine?" His brother stared at him as if he had lost his mind.

"Yes! If you had never made us start this foolish scheme of avoiding Mama, she—"

"She would have done exactly as she has done. *We* have nothing to do with it." Nick's tone was bitter.

"Perhaps she was lonely without us, and . . ."

"Did she *seem* lonely?"

William was forced to shake his head.

"I tell you, we didn't matter a whit," insisted Nicholas, his delicate face flushed with hurt and anger. He was valiantly suppressing tears. "No one cares for us anymore."

William set his jaw to keep it from trembling.

"Well, I *won't*," exclaimed Susan, stamping her small foot, her green eyes blazing with rage.

"Won't what?" responded her brothers simultaneously.

"I won't marry that . . . that awful man. He doesn't like us."

"You can't tell whether—"

"I can so! I saw how he looked at me, at all of us. He doesn't like us at all."

Thinking back to their one meeting with Sir Charles, the boys frowned. There was something in what Susan said. They had all sensed that Norbury was not interested in them. "Well, you're not the one who is marrying him," replied Nicholas pessimistically. "Mama is, and there is nothing we can do about it."

"Is there not?" His sister's eyes blazed.

"Susan, what are you thinking of?" The boys exchanged an apprehensive glance.

The little girl gazed at them with irate contempt. "I shall—"

Her answer was cut off by the reappearance of the governess, who, knowing nothing of what had passed, was calmly determined to return to lessons. William and Nicholas obeyed resignedly, but Susan continued to glower at her book for the rest of the morning.

Chapter Nine

When Christopher Hanford came down to breakfast the next morning, his sister was already sitting at the table, poring over the freshly arrived edition of the *Morning Post*. She was so engrossed that she did not hear his approach, but when he pulled out a chair and sat opposite, she started violently and swept the newspaper onto the floor with a convulsive gesture, gazing at him with wide, apprehensive eyes.

"Did I startle you? I'm sorry," he said. He lifted the lid off a silver dish. "Muffins!"

His sister made no effort to retrieve the paper. She continued to stare, then, recovering herself, looked hastily at her plate. But her fork remained forgotten beside it.

"I'm going riding with the Wyndhams today," added Christopher, helping himself to tea. "*All* of them." He looked very cheerful at the thought. "We used to ride together often at home."

Amelia made a small stifled noise.

"It's not so pleasant in London, of course—no space for a real gallop. But I daresay we shall have a fine time nonetheless." He buttered a hot muffin liberally, glancing up. "Is something wrong, Amelia? You look pale."

"No, no. I'm perfectly well."

He nodded and bit into the muffin. "Have you finished with the newspaper? I should like to see it if you have."

"No! I mean . . ." She looked down at the crumpled pages on the carpet. She could hardly claim she was reading. "It . . . it is sadly dull today."

Her brother eyed her quizzically.

Amelia frowned. She did not want him to see the announcement. It would make him so unhappy. Yet he would have to know sometime. And if Anabel Wyndham mentioned her engagement while they were riding today, and he found out then . . . With a sigh she bent and reached for the paper, handing it to him. It was already folded to the relevant page, and Amelia watched as he spread it out on the table, sipping his tea, and began to scan the announcements. She couldn't look away.

At first Hanford read with a slight smile. The reported doings of society always amused him. But when his eyes reached the middle of the second column, his face suddenly froze. He leaned forward, read again, and looked up at his sister, stricken.

Amelia met his blue eyes with sympathy, then with surprise at what she saw there. She had expected chagrin, disappointment, perhaps anger. She had been ready to comfort and condole. But she had always thought of her brother as a self-sufficient and imperturbable person, not bothered by depths of feeling. Even as a child he had always seemed untouched by emotion, and Amelia, five years younger, had often been annoyed by his bland competence. Now she realized that she had been wrong. The anguish in Christopher's eyes was unmistakable. All of his calm authority was gone. He even looked different— the set of his shoulders and lines in his face had shifted so that he seemed almost a stranger. "I'm so sorry, Christopher," she murmured. "I know you . . ."

"I have lost her, Amelia," he said. He gazed at her with a bewildered hurt she had never thought to see. "What shall I do?"

Amelia bit her lower lip. She had always been the one who asked advice. Many people relied on Christopher so, she knew. It was disconcerting to have the tables turned and see her invincible brother at a loss. But after a moment's uncertainty she straightened, determined to help him in the way he had helped her so often. "It is only an engagement, Christopher. Engagements are broken every day."

"Not by Anabel. She is not that sort." He bent his head and rested it on his palm. The shock of seeing Anabel's name publicly linked to Norbury's had not worn off.

"She is dazzled by Norbury's manner," suggested Amelia, hoping she was right. "It will wear thin, you will see."

"When she is married to him?" he retorted bitterly. "When it is too late? That is worse still."

His sister grimaced. She thought this scenario only too likely, but she did not wish to increase his unhappiness. "Perhaps before. You must not give up, Christopher. Anabel will see—"

"See?" He laughed harshly. "In nearly four years she has *seen* nothing. I have tried in every way I know to show her my love, and she has taken it as a matter of course, as mere friendship! Good old Christopher! Reliable Christopher! And the moment she meets a posturing, arrogant Londoner, she . . ." He threw himself back in his chair and expelled a despairing sigh. "She doesn't care for me, Amelia. It's obvious."

"She does. She is always so glad to see you."

"As a friend, yes. As someone who will help her out of scrapes and tidy up her tangles. But not as a man to love."

He put a hand to his eyes again, furiously dashing away a hint of moisture there. "Perhaps I should just go home. I don't belong in town."

"Oh, Christopher!" She rose and went around the table to embrace him. "It is not so hopeless. You are exaggerating. I don't think Anabel knows *what* she feels. And I don't think you should give up so easily."

Hanford put his hand over hers on his shoulder and patted it. "You are trying to be kind, I know, Amelia. But perhaps I would be better off out of this."

She hesitated, wondering if he were right, then shook her head. In his country house, alone, he would only lose himself in his miseries. "No, you must stay, and wait. I have a feeling something will happen."

He smiled slightly. "A feeling? Am I to risk my happiness on so thin a support?"

"My feelings very often turn out true," she insisted, drawing back a little to look at him.

Christopher gazed up at her. "But I do not know if I can bear it, watching her with him, seeing the whole *ton* acknowledge their engagement. She will expect me to be glad for her. I . . ." His voice broke, and he stopped, clearing his throat.

His anguished expression struck Amelia to the heart. "Oh, my dear," she said, embracing him again. "I am so sorry!"

They remained thus for a long moment, then Christopher straightened and she stepped back. He was staring at the wall as if it told him something. "I wonder what the children said when she told them?" He turned to Amelia. "Norbury doesn't care for them."

"He wouldn't."

Hanford set his jaw. "Perhaps you are right. Perhaps I should stay for a while. It will be damnably difficult, but I suppose I can manage it. If she should change her mind . . ." A muscle jumped in his cheek. "But I shan't hope for that. I shall just make certain that they are *all* happy with the change, and then I shall go home."

Amelia wondered if he were deceiving himself about his motive, but she said nothing to alter his decision. She had her own ideas about Anabel's attachment, ideas that were difficult to state and impossible to prove, and she thought it likely that there would be further developments before any wedding took place.

"I have to get ready to go out," her brother added. "How can I take them riding after *this*?" He struck the newspaper with the back of his hand. "I feel like shaking her."

"It might do her a great deal of good," replied Amelia.

Christopher smiled, shaking his head. "I will have to devote myself to the children to keep my temper."

That would be a very wise thing to do, agreed Amelia, but not aloud. She watched her brother walk out of the room, then abandoned her half-finished breakfast to hurry to the morning room and write a note.

The Wyndham family was ready and eager when Christopher arrived at their door an hour later. The children jumped up and down with impatience at the sight of the hired horses he and a groom had brought from the livery, and Anabel held out her hand with a smile. He hardly knew how he answered, but somehow they mounted and set off, one of Lady Goring's grooms joining the other behind them.

"We are fortunate to have such a fine day," said Anabel. The sun was shining, and a soft breeze was refreshing without being cold.

"Yes," he agreed. He was finding it difficult to look at her, and talking was out of the question. He wanted to rail, to accuse, but he had no right. Luckily Susan dropped back beside them, her pony diminutive beside Hanford's roan.

"I want to see where *you* live," she demanded of him.

He smiled down at her determined little face. The sun made Susan's red hair brillant, and her green eyes sparkled. "I thought you wanted to go to the park."

"Yes. Afterward."

He laughed. "Well, we can ride past the house, I suppose. It is not far out of the way. But we are *not* going in."

Susan nodded, satisfied. Hanford called to the two boys, who had ridden a little ahead, and the party turned right at the next street, riding past the Lanforth town house. Susan gazed around her with intense interest and eyed the facade as if memorizing it. Then, abruptly, she declared she was ready to go on. Her brothers sighed with relief; they had been afraid she would drag them to some other dull place. And the adults exchanged a smile. For a moment Christopher felt happy, then he remembered the engagement and urged his mount forward.

"You're quiet today," he said to William and Nicholas when he came up with them.

William shrugged. Nick said, "We're thinking. Have you heard that Mama is getting married?"

Feeling as if he had taken a blow to the chest, Hanford nodded.

"Well, we're wondering what we can do about it."

William snorted derisively.

"Do?" Hanford felt a bit guilty inquiring. He had no right to interfere, he knew, but he couldn't resist finding out the children's attitude toward the match.

"To stop her. She is to marry that Norbury, you know."

"Yes."

"We don't like him!"

"Don't be an idiot, Nick," put in William. "There's nothing we can do."

"Not if we don't even try!" replied his brother hotly.

Hanford's intense gratification at their remarks made him more uneasy. He should not be talking so to Anabel's children, yet it was hard to resist.

"Do *you* like him?" asked Nicholas with a frown.

"I?" Christopher was at a loss. "I . . . I scarcely know him."

"I didn't think so." The boy nodded, satisfied. "There's something wrong with him. Even Susan sees it."

"I didn't mean . . ." Hanford groped for words. He didn't want to lie, but neither could he in conscience encourage Nick.

"I shall think of something," was the younger Wyndham's only response.

They reached the gates of the park, and Anabel and Susan caught up with them so that they entered in a group. The children immediately kicked their mounts' flanks and trotted off at the fastest pace allowed in this fashionable enclosure. Christopher and Anabel watched them.

"It was so good of you to think of this," she said, "I don't know why I didn't myself. They love riding so."

"They're very good at it, too."

"I hope so. They certainly don't take much care. I have scolded them about it over and over."

He gazed after the three bouncing children. There was no chance of a neck-or-nothing gallop here, but they were throwing themselves into their more sedate progress. William had a fine seat and good hands; Nick, though slightly less skilled, clearly made up for it in spirit, and Susan showed all the signs of a future belle of the hunt. She would be the kind of rider, Hanford thought, who drives the young men frantic in their efforts to keep up and surpass her. Few would manage the thing.

"Uncle Christopher!" called Nick. "Come on." He signaled vigorously.

Smiling, Hanford rode forward to join them. He noticed that they did not summon their mother. In another moment he was pulled into a lively game of follow-the-leader, each rider having to imitate the antics of the first. The children's attempts to find some new challenge made him laugh so that he almost forgot Anabel.

She was watching from nearby, smiling at first at the way they were all enjoying themselves, then, gradually, becoming pensive. None of them shouted to draw her attention to some particularly astonishing trick. They didn't ask for her approval or arbitration of a dispute. They hardly looked in her direction. Her own children and her dearest friend gamboled there, and ignored her. In the past this would have been unimaginable. She would have laughed at anyone who suggested the possibility. But it was happening now. Slowly the sight of them grew oppressive. Had they forgotten she was here? Even Susan, squealing with delight as she played leader and forced the males into the most ridiculous contortions, did not turn wickedly sparkling green eyes for her approval. Anabel drooped a little in her saddle.

She knew the children were not pleased about her engagement, but now that she thought about it, she realized they had been rather aloof for some time. The close, easy relationship that had always existed in her family was breaking down. And Christopher—he must have seen the announcement in the *Morning Post*, but he had not even wished her happy. He had been cold lately, too.

Anabel felt very isolated, sitting on her horse and watching the others cavort. It seemed to her suddenly that she had no one. Her old life was shutting her out, and the new one had not yet developed to take its place. Tears of self-pity started in her eyes. But before one could drop, she shook her head and kicked her horse's flanks. She was being ridiculous. "May I join the game?" she called in the gayest tone she could muster.

"We've just finished," answered Nick. "Susan won. We're going to ride down that avenue now and see what's on the other side of the park."

With that, they all started off, leaving Anabel to follow in their wake. Christopher felt another wave of guilt as he rode. He shouldn't encourage the children to show their displeasure so openly. But he hadn't actually urged them; he had simply gone along with their schemes. And since he agreed wholeheartedly with their reaction, he felt his behavior was sufficiently justified. He was no self-sacrificing martyr, to argue against his own interests.

All in all, the riding party could not be called a success. They explored the lanes of the park for another hour, the children chattering to one another and to Christopher but speaking to Anabel only when directly addressed. Hanford exchanged commonplaces with her, unable to mention the engagement, and she grew more and more silent and withdrawn as the morning progressed. Everyone seemed relieved when they turned toward home again.

They rode back on one of the more-traveled avenues of the park, by this time filling with members of the *haut ton*, and their pace slowed perforce. Christopher soon noticed that Anabel was attracting a great deal of attention. Elegantly dressed ladies in smart barouches whispered among themselves as they nodded greetings. Pinks on horseback eyed her with speculative appraisal. Here is the woman, their eyes all said, who won the unconquerable Norbury. What is so special about her? How did she manage it?

Anabel saw it, too, and found her new notoriety dreadful. It had been bad enough when everyone was wondering if Norbury would propose; now the attention was redoubled, and she hated it. "Why are we dawdling like this?" she said, moving forward and almost colliding with a landaulet.

The children looked mystified—all morning she had been urging them to slow down—but Christopher understood, and even his anger with her could not prevent sympathy.

"Yes, we should be getting back," he agreed, guiding them around the carriage and toward the gate.

The ride through the streets was generally silent. The children went on ahead, and Anabel was too occupied with her own thoughts to talk. When he left the Wyndhams at Lady Goring's house, Christopher was thoughtful. Perhaps Amelia had been right. There might be developments before the wedding took place. He would stay in town a while yet.

Anabel, walking up the steps and into the front hall, was wondering how she could excuse herself from going to the play tonight. They had planned the evening some time ago, and Georgina was very eager to see the melodrama, she knew. But could she not plead a headache and stay home alone? She dreaded facing the curious stares and whispered evaluations of the crowd in the playhouse.

In the event, she could not. Lady Goring was called to the bedside of one of the servants just after dinner, and the girl was ill enough that she felt she should stay with her until the doctor came. "I will join you later, if I can," she told Anabel and Georgina. "It is only some trifling thing, no doubt, but Nancy is terrified of the doctor, and I want to make sure she sees him."

"Perhaps we should all stay," ventured Anabel.

Georgina looked desolate.

"Nonsense. There is nothing for you to do. Go on and enjoy the play. I daresay I shall come in before the second act."

Meeting her cousin's eyes, Anabel could not refuse to go. Thus, the two of them set out together soon after, Georgina chattering about the play and Anabel morosely silent.

106

They entered their box in good time. Georgina had insisted they come well before the curtain. Anabel sat down and glanced quickly around, holding herself very straight. At least she could be confident about her appearance. She had put on a new gown of soft rose satin, which she had fallen in love with at the dressmaker's shop. The cloth seemed to shimmer with a dusting of muted silver, and she had had it cut with a scoop at the neck, tiny puffed sleeves, and a wide ruffle around the hem. It clung to the curves of her body with just the proper mixture of enticement and propriety, and looked lovely with a set of silver filigree that had belonged to Ralph's mother. None of the gapers could claim that she *looked* peaked or out of sorts, though she felt far from confident.

Georgina was gazing eagerly about the theater, smiling at people she knew and flushing with pleasure when some of the young men she had danced with saluted their box. The girl's happiness had been increasing with each new day of the season, as she received further proofs of her attractiveness and gained poise. "There are the Leamingtons," she said. "Oh, I hope George will come by at the interval. I want to tell Sophie about the rout party on Thursday. She had the headache and missed it."

Anabel did not look up. Her interest in the Leamingtons was minimal. She instead wished that the play would begin so that she could retreat into dimness. For it was obvious that their box was attracting attention. People indicated it to their friends with pointed glances, then bent to murmur comments to one another. It was worse than in the park.

At last the curtain rose. Georgina leaned forward and became absorbed, and Anabel relaxed a little, letting her rigid back and fixed smile slip. She fervently hoped that her mother would indeed join them, though she knew it was unlikely. But Lady Goring's sensible presence would be a great help tonight. She would not hesitate to face down anyone ill bred enough to stare. She would fix them with her lorgnette and raised eyebrows until they retreated in embarrassment. The picture amused Anabel and elicited a real smile, making her feel a little better. The *ton*'s avid interest would pass, she told herself; some new sensation would arise, and she would be forgotten. She need only endure.

Lady Goring did not arrive, and at the first interval several of Georgina's new friends stopped by the box to chat with her. Anabel gratefully retreated to the rear and left them to it, marveling at the change in her cousin since her first days in London. Who would connect that pallid, sullen girl with the laughing, almost slender one before her now? Georgina was not beautiful, but she was far from ugly. Her well-shaped face and fine gray eyes were transformed by expression. Happy, she was very engaging.

"Contemplating the merits of the play?" asked a voice near her ear.

Anabel started and turned to find Sir Charles beside her.

"You looked very thoughtful," he added, "and not well pleased. My opinion precisely."

She smiled. "I wasn't thinking about the play."

"No? What, then?" His eyes caressed her.

"Nothing. Georgina."

Norbury glanced briefly at the girl, then dismissed her. "Alas. You might have been thinking of me."

"I have been. I could hardly help it." This didn't sound just right, she realized at once. She hadn't meant to be tart.

Norbury wasn't offended, however. "There has been some reaction," he agreed. "Only natural. The *ton* has so little to occupy it."

"It's . . . rather unpleasant." It was good to have someone to share her discomfort.

"You don't find it amusing to set their silly tongues wagging?" He looked around the theater with a superior smile. Their tête-à-tête was the center of many eyes. "But we are practically social benefactors. They would be so deucedly dull without us."

Anabel tried to smile, but his joke seemed sadly flat tonight. "I don't seem to have the character for philanthropy."

"Nonsense." He laughed. With the air of a man turning from trivial to important things, he added, "I have arranged our visit to Kent. My mother is delighted; she is very eager to meet you. We go down on Wednesday."

"Oh." Anabel felt a bit annoyed at his assumption that she could leave whenever he chose. "I believe we were engaged for dinner on Wednesday."

He waved this aside. "It is far more important that you become acquainted with my family."

She frowned and started to protest, but the interval was ending. People had returned to their seats, and the curtain was about to rise again.

"I will remain here with you," said Norbury with a smile. "There appears to be an empty chair." And in the dimness that followed the resumption of the play, his hand curled over hers in her lap. Anabel stirred a little, afraid the gossips would see. But the theater was too dark.

Throughout the second act, with Charles' fingers warm and suggestive around hers, she tried to analyze her feelings. The day had been far from satisfactory. She had been shaken first by her novel isolation from the children and Christopher, then by the half-malicious scrutiny of the *ton*. Now, with Charles at her side to support her, she ought to feel better, she thought. Love was supposed to overcome all sorts of ills; she was his acknowledged choice, the envy of many less fortunate women. Why, then, did she still feel dispirited and uneasy? Glancing over at Charles in the dim light, she traced the handsome contours of his face. *He* looked supremely confident and content. Perhaps it was just that she was unused to town life. The furor would decline, and surely the children would come round when they became accustomed to the idea of her marriage and knew Charles better. She must see to that.

When the second interval was announced, Anabel spoke first. "You must come to dinner with the children. Mama mentioned it. What about tomorrow night?"

Norbury's smile faded. "I have an engagement tomorrow."

"Oh. Sunday, then?" When he hesitated, she added, "You must get to know them better. They are not . . . wholly reconciled to the idea of my marrying again."

He frowned. "What has it to do with them?"

"Well, Charles . . ." She searched for words, astonished by his reaction. "We will be one family, after all."

Hearing the doubt and amazement in her voice, he shrugged. "Of course. You must make allowances for the fact that I know nothing of children." He had released her hand, but now he bent closer. "Though I hope to learn a great deal very soon." His eyes were provocative, and she could not mistake that look for interest in her own children.

"You will come, then?" she replied a bit stiffly.

"Yes." He smiled, and she told herself that all would be well when he and the children were better acquainted.

Norbury escorted them to their carriage at the end of the play. They were repeatedly detained by other members of the audience offering congratulations and full of questions about their plans. Anabel left the answers to him, though she was not always in agreement with them, because she could not face the innumerable pairs of avid eyes and falsely smiling mouths. None of these people truly wished them happiness, she felt; indeed, they would be much more interested in the opposite. And they inquired only to have news to retail to other, less-informed friends. There was no warmth in their faces.

Norbury didn't seem to care. He took patent pleasure in accepting their good wishes and dropping carefully rationed bits of information to one or the other. He was in his element, Anabel thought, without admitting the implications of their very different responses to the situation.

As he handed her into her carriage he dropped a light kiss on her wrist. "Shall I see you tomorrow at the Atleys'?"

"No." Anabel felt she couldn't bear another such evening. "I must . . . help Mama."

This was weak, and he raised his eyebrows. "Help?"

"Yes." She pulled the carriage door, and he shut it. "We will meet at dinner on Sunday."

"Ah. Yes."

"Good night." She smiled and drew back. After a moment he stepped away and signaled the coachman to start. Anabel sighed with relief, very glad to see the end of this evening. She had been longing for the quiet of her bedchamber for hours.

But once there and in her dressing gown, she remained restless. The days ahead seemed full of difficult tasks and unwelcome events. For the first time since the season had started, she wished she was back home. There, she had never felt so alone or endured a day like this one. She had been surrounded by family and friends, secure in their undoubted affection. She had not been plagued by decisions and worry over whether she had decided correctly. Perhaps she should never have come to London.

Then, climbing into bed, she shook her head slightly and scolded herself for cowardice. Things could not remain always the same. The children were growing up alarmingly quickly, and in a few years she would have been alone in the country as well. It was time she took charge of her life, and she would become accustomed to the process eventually, she had no doubt. In any case, things always looked better in the morning.

Chapter Ten

Anabel did not see Sir Charles again until the evening set for dinner. Indeed, she did not go out on Saturday, having had her fill of unwanted attention. Lady Goring was once again available to chaperone Georgina, and Anabel left them to attend a ball while she stayed home with her thoughts. She spent the early evening in the schoolroom with the children, trying to recapture their old intimacy, and partly succeeding. They could not resist her affectionate overtures. But a pall remained over the family, and the younger Wyndhams showed a notable lack of enthusiasm when told that Norbury was coming to meet them.

He arrived punctually at six, and Anabel, who had been on the watch, came downstairs as the footman let him in. The atmosphere in the drawing room was stiff, and she wanted to take him in herself.

"Good evening," he said, handing his hat and gloves to the servant and offering her his arm. "Here I am, as commanded. Do you know, I have never in my life eaten my dinner at six. It will be a novel experience."

"The children always eat early," answered Anabel, a little piqued by his mocking tone.

"Of course."

They walked up the stairs together.

"They . . . they are still becoming accustomed to the idea of our marriage," she added in a rush. "You must understand if they are . . . a bit . . . wary at first."

"Ah?" He raised one dark eyebrow, not helping her.

"It is difficult for children to adjust to new arrangements, you know. They like everything to stay as it was."

"Indeed? And I thought I had been told they were very flexible creatures. My mistake, I imagine."

Anabel frowned. No one was making it easy for her. She felt like a clumsy diplomat, trying to negotiate between warring states. Her mother had been elaborately bland about the evening, and Georgina didn't seem to understand how awkward it might be.

They entered the drawing room. "You know my mother, of course," said Anabel. "And I believe you have met my cousin Georgina Goring." Norbury nodded. "And this is William." The children had been thoroughly coached. William came forward and made his bow. "Nicholas." The younger boy followed suit. "And the youngest, Susan." Susan curtsied, but her expression remained sullen.

"How do you do?" replied Norbury, smiling dutifully.

There was a short silence.

"Shall we sit down?" said Anabel, feeling desperate. She had not realized until this moment what divergent topics of conversation she used with Norbury, the children, and even her mother. None of them was interested in the others' favorite subjects. She could not imagine Charles discussing a new pony for Susan, or William's dogs, nor her mother enduring Norbury's gibes at society in silence. She had to say something, but she couldn't think of any neutral topic that would include them all.

"You boys are not at school?" inquired Sir Charles with a geniality that did not conceal his boredom.

William glanced quickly at his mother, then shook his head.

"Taking a holiday?"

"We don't go to school," responded Nicholas. "Mama teaches us. Or, she did. *Now* we have a governess."

"Really?" His eyebrow cocked again, Norbury turned to Anabel. "Do you think that wise? Boys are usually better off at school."

The children glowered, and Anabel felt a spark of resentment. "I have considered sending them. They are very young yet."

"They look like well grown lads to me." He attempted joviality again. "And I daresay they wish they were in school with other boys. Don't you?"

William and Nicholas simply scowled. Lady Goring watched the scene with interest, her expression bland but her eyes sparkling. Georgina was looking from one to another of the group with the dawning apprehension that something was wrong.

"Well, well," added Norbury, sensing opposition. "We can talk of that another time. Tell me, William, are you fond of hunting?"

Though riding out with the local hunt was one of William's passions, he shrugged.

"No? I would have pegged you as a bruising rider. What about Nicholas?"

Seeing his mother's pained expression, Nicholas relented and admitted they liked to hunt.

"I have a hunting box in Leicestershire," replied Norbury. "We had some splendid runs last season."

In any other circumstances the boys would have pelted him with eager questions about the Quorn, but Norbury's position in the family, and the fact that he made no move to invite them to hunt with him or even to suggest that they might at some future time, left them silent.

Sir Charles, annoyed at their unresponsiveness, turned to Susan. "And what do you like?" he asked. "I suppose you have a great many . . . dolls?"

His tone was condescending, and Susan, who had one much-beloved rag doll and a host of less important ones, pursed her small mouth and shook her head. "I hate dolls!"

Norbury raised his eyebrows again.

"I believe dinner must be ready," blurted Anabel, looking beseechingly at her mother.

Lady Goring had been letting events take their course with some satisfaction, but now she took pity on her daughter. "Yes, I think we might go in." Rising, she took Norbury's arm and started toward the dining room. "Did you notice Julia Buckingham's new town carriage at the ball last night, Sir Charles?" she asked. "That's the third this year, is it not? I hope Buckingham can stand the nonsense."

Norbury responded wittily, and the first half of the meal passed in similar remarks between the two. He repeatedly sought to bring Anabel into the conversation, but she was too conscious of the children, silent and ignored, eating their dinner without looking up from their plates. Georgina occasionally spoke to them, but tonight she elicited no more than monosyllables.

With the second course came another silence. Lady Goring had exhausted her fund of gossip, and in any case she wished to give her daughter another dose of reality. She addressed herself to a Chantilly cream. "This is very fine, isn't it, William?" she said.

William, who was fond of sweets, nodded enthusiastically.

"I forgot to ask. Did you have a good ride in the park on Friday? Were the horses from the livery suitable?"

"They were slugs," answered Nicholas. "But better than

nothing. We had some first-class games with Uncle Christopher."

"Yes," seconded William heartily.

"We like Uncle Christopher better than *anybody*," offered Susan.

Her brothers seemed to feel that this was going too far. They fell silent again and concentrated on their plates.

" 'Uncle' Christopher?" queried Norbury. "Ah. That would be the fellow I met here one day. Hanford, wasn't it? One of your bucolic neighbors."

His tone made Anabel's cheeks redden slightly. But before she could reply, Georgina snapped, "He is a wonderful man!"

"Is he?" Norbury eyed her with cool amusement. "I must become better acquainted with him."

Georgina turned fiery red and looked down.

"He is a good friend and a close neighbor," said Anabel. "I don't know what I would have done without him when Ralph died."

"Indeed?" He looked less pleased.

"Shall we remove to the drawing room?" asked Lady Goring. She was happy to see Anabel learning some home truths about Norbury, but she had no intention of letting things get out of hand. "You must come with us, Sir Charles. We are a household of females and have no proper port."

They returned to the drawing room, and the children went to bed soon after, followed by Georgina. At this, the situation eased somewhat, and Anabel found conversation easier. But when Lady Goring excused herself a little later and Charles came to sit close beside her on the sofa, she was not in the mood for dalliance. "It didn't go particularly well," she said.

"What?" He seemed honestly puzzled.

"The dinner. I had hoped you and the children would . . . like one another."

"Like?" He frowned in perplexity. "I daresay we shall rub along quite well eventually. The boys must go off to school, of course; it is past time. And as for Susan"—he smiled provocatively at her—"I have not yet encountered the female I could not captivate." His arm tightened around her shoulders.

Thinking that he was unlikely to have encountered one like her daughter, Anabel sat very straight. "I am not sure I wish to send them to school. I put it off because I wanted them with me."

He shrugged, smiling. "There is no need to discuss it now. You will be making a great many changes. Pleasant ones, I hope." Bending his head, he kissed her.

Gradually Anabel relaxed against his arm, feeling again that languorous helplessness Charles always produced in her. His free hand wandered along her silk-clad body, and slowly she brought one arm up and about his neck. The kiss seemed to go on forever. Anabel's annoyance and objections slipped from her mind; she felt reasonless, without volition.

When he drew back, he was breathing rapidly, his hand at rest on her hip. "Lovely Anabel," he murmured. "Do you know how I love you? There is no woman like you in the world."

She gazed into his pale green eyes, still tremulous from his caress. He cared about her. It was obvious. But what did *she* feel, beyond that pliant loss of will? She was less and less certain, and that fact was increasingly unsettling. "It's late," she said.

He laughed a little. "Don't you trust me? You can, you know. And that is more than could be said for almost any woman I have known. Do you feel your power?" He pulled her closer and kissed her again, then straightened and rose. "I will go, with great reluctance. We must set a wedding date, Anabel. Very soon."

"I . . . I haven't thought."

He laughed again. "Well, do so, my heart's darling. Think very hard." He took her hand and kissed the palm. "And dream of me." With a last flashing smile, he went out.

She looked at her hand for a moment, then let it fall and suddenly shivered. She didn't understand anything anymore, least of all herself. Events seemed to be rushing forward, out of control. She knew she had to do something, but what? She didn't even know what she wanted. She had thought she did; she had been dazzled by possibilities and new sensations. Now nothing was clear. Her brain seemed to whirl dizzyingly from one image to another, never pausing long enough for her to really see any. Her emotions were in turmoil. And no one could help her.

With a sigh, Anabel turned toward the stairs. She would have difficulty sleeping again tonight, she could tell. But it did no good to stand here and worry. Perhaps time would solve her problems for her.

The following day was very quiet in Lady Goring's household. Anabel did not go out. She prepared for her journey to Kent and spent a great deal of time sitting and thinking. In the afternoon she went up to the schoolroom to tell the children she would be away for a short time, and met the predictable unenthusiastic response. As she was coming down the stairs again she encountered Georgina, dressed for the street and accompanied by her maid. She looked excited. "Are you going out?" asked Anabel.

"Yes." The girl smiled. "I am invited to tea with Amelia Lanforth. It is so close that I am going to walk."

Anabel felt chagrin. Why was her cousin asked to the Lanforths and not she? She had known Christopher for years, certainly his sister might have included her in the invitation. They had chatted at several gatherings, and though they had never had an opportunity to become well acquainted, Anabel liked Mrs. Lanforth very much. She would have been happy to see her more intimately. Had Christopher's inexplicable new coldness spread to his sister? She frowned.

"I must go," added Georgina. "I don't want to be late." And with a sense of half-guilty relief, she skipped past and down to the hall. Georgina was finding Anabel puzzling lately. Her older cousin seemed either abstracted or overanimated, and the previous evening had been dreadful.

At the Lanforths, Georgina was taken directly up to the drawing room and greeted with a smile by Amelia. They had confirmed their mutual passion for novels during a visit Amelia had made to Lady Goring after the announcement of Anabel's engagement, and they both looked forward to a long, cozy chat comparing all their favorites.

They settled on the sofa and fortified themselves with cups of strong tea. But before they could really begin, the drawing-room door opened and Christopher came in. Georgina's eyes brightened, and her cup rattled slightly in its saucer.

"Christopher," said Amelia. "I thought you had gone out riding."

"Yes. But I returned early. The park is too crowded. Will you give me some tea?" He smiled also, but his voice and stance conveyed depression.

"Of course." She poured out another cup. "But I give you fair warning we mean to talk about novels. We have met just for that purpose, and you won't stop us."

Hanford's smile became more genuine. "Ah. Didn't I tell you, Miss Goring, that my sister's interest in them equaled your own?"

Georgina nodded, speechless with joy at his joining them.

"And do you have favorites in common?" he added.

"We haven't discovered that yet." Amelia smiled at the girl. "I am excessively attached to Mrs. Radcliffe."

"Oh, yes! I have never been so frightened as when the wicked duke . . ." They fell into an energetic exchange, and Christopher allowed their voices to fade into a background for his thoughts. Despite his resolutions, he was finding it extremely difficult to remain in London. He thought of nothing but Anabel, though he rarely saw her. And he had nothing to do. At home he would manage his estate and ride out every day. Here there were only parties which reminded him again of his loss. He didn't know how much longer he could endure it.

"Yes, I was reading it only last night before Sir Charles came to dinner," said Georgina.

Hanford looked up. "Norbury came to dinner yesterday?"

She turned to him. "Yes. Anabel wanted him to meet the children and . . . become friends." Her tone was so doubtful that both her listeners understood the attempt had not met with success. Christopher felt a rush of guilty joy.

"I suppose the children are not very pleased about the engagement," said Amelia. And as the others looked at her she added, "They rarely are in such cases. It is a great change."

Georgina, frowning over this novel viewpoint, slowly nodded. "I think you are right. I have never seen them so sullen as last night. Of course, Sir Charles did not help. He does not know how to talk to children."

This naïve statement made Amelia smile and Christopher lean forward, unconsciously avid. Georgina noticed it, and compared his earlier despondence with the intense eagerness in his eyes now. A revelation swept over her, and she sat back abruptly, stricken.

"I admit I do not see how they will go on together," said Hanford. "Norbury is settled in London. He goes into the country only to visit or hunt. But I cannot imagine Anabel or the children staying here permanently."

"He . . . he means to send the boys to school," managed Georgina. Her throat seemed to be obstructed by a large lump.

"School. Well, it is time they went. But I should have thought Anabel would want to decide. Is she going to let him take over her life?" This last came out charged with emotion and, realizing it, Christopher shut his mouth and turned a little away.

Georgina scanned his profile and wondered at the confusion of emotions she felt. It hurt to discover that the man she so admired was in love with someone else; yet she could not help but see the logic of it. He had known Anabel for years, and her cousin was very lovely and charming. To her own surprise, she realized that her strongest response was pity. She wished she could do something to comfort Hanford and to change things so that he might be happy. She loved him, but . . . "I . . . I think Anabel was a little annoyed with him when he suggested it," she ventured.

Amelia, hearing the quaver in her voice, looked sharply at her. What she saw made her eyes soften and a slight smile curve her lips. Unconsciously she reached over and patted the girl's hand. When Georgina looked up, startled, she said, "More tea?" knowing that to acknowledge the girl's state would be unforgivable.

Georgina shook her head, turning back to Christopher.

"Annoyed? Was she really?" he could not resist asking.

"Yes. It was not at all a pleasant evening." She wanted desperately to cheer him.

"Ah."

"And I heard Lady Goring say that Sir Charles' mother is disagreeable. So perhaps when Anabel goes to Kent to visit her—"

"She is going out of town?"

"Yes. Tomorrow. But only for a day."

Hanford leaned his head on his hand briefly, then straightened. "I beg your pardon. I have remembered something I must do. Please excuse me." He left the room in three strides, the women silent behind him. Georgina anxiously watched the door close, and Amelia watched her.

"Will he be all right?" the girl asked finally.

Amelia shrugged.

"It is so . . . I didn't know . . . I would never have . . ."

"You did splendidly," Amelia assured her. "Your aunt— and your father, no doubt—would be proud of you. Indeed, I am."

Georgina frowned doubtfully at her, biting her lower lip. She felt exposed.

Amelia bent to pour more tea. "But you were telling me about a new book you have found. I must hear all about it. I have been searching for something fresh to read this age."

Georgina took a deep breath and tried to gather her thoughts. What book had she been talking about? She had no idea.

"Was it called *The Count's Revenge*?" prompted Amelia.

"Oh. Oh, yes." And with a massive effort she took up her description again.

In the library downstairs, Christopher sat alone, head bent. Anabel was going away; she had freely accepted another man, and she continued to ignore his feelings. He had never felt so low in his life as he did at that moment. All hope of happiness seemed gone. He would gladly have throttled Sir Charles Norbury, but he had no excuse to do so. The children's dislike was no motive. Anabel liked him—loved him!—and that tied his hands and racked his heart.

Chapter Eleven

Anabel departed for the visit to Norbury's family at ten the following morning. She was not at all eager to make the journey, feeling that many things required her attention at home, but she had agreed to go and Charles seemed set on it. As they would spend only one night at his mother's and return the following afternoon, she made no objections when he arrived in his traveling carriage and handed her in.

The drive was about three hours, and during it Charles was once again the charming, sophisticated companion she had admired at *ton* parties. He did not make love to her; rather, he pointed out sights along their route, reminisced about his childhood trips on that road, and asked her opinion about various arrangements he had made. Before long she was feeling more in charity with him than she had for a while, and she laughed at his sallies unrestrainedly.

"You have told me nothing about your family," she said as they began the last stage of the journey. "I know I am to meet your mother. Will there be others as well?"

"I fear so. My marriage is such an astonishing development that every ambulatory Norbury has gathered to witness the miracle." He looked comical, and she laughed again.

"But who is that? You must prepare me."

"I dare not. You might simply jump out of the chaise and leave me to face them alone."

"Perhaps I shall if you keep me wondering what I am in for."

Norbury smiled. "Very well. Besides my mother, whom you will like very much, I think, there will be two uncles with their families. One is my late father's younger brother and the other my mother's older one. Enough?"

"Not at all. How many cousins?"

He groaned. "Three. But we are fortunate. There are three more who will not be present for one reason or another."

"You don't get on with them?"

"We cordially despise one another, and have since we were in short coats."

Anabel looked doubtful; this didn't sound like a happy family.

"Don't judge until you have met them," added Norbury.

After a moment she nodded. "Have you no brothers or sisters?"

"None. The explanation, according to one of my uncles, of all my character flaws. Overindulgence."

"You are making me dread this visit, Charles."

"You asked to be warned. You see I am being completely honest with you." He grinned. "It is unlike me."

"Well, I think you are teasing me. They are probably all very pleasant people."

He smiled. "You may decide for yourself. Here we are."

Anabel looked out the window. They had turned in at a massive stone gate and were trotting up an avenue lined with oaks. At the end, she could see a pillared portico of gray stone, windows glittering in the afternoon sun. Well-kept gardens extended around the sides to the back, and the place had an air of carefully controlled wealth. She turned back, to find Norbury gazing at her expectantly. "It is beautiful."

"Is it not? Your new home."

Inevitably this made Anabel think of the less grand but comfortable and familiar house she had left behind. It would be very hard to abandon it for this.

They pulled up to the front door with a flourish, and it opened before they could climb down. A liveried footman ushered them into the hall and took their wraps as another fetched the luggage and a third waited to escort them farther into the house. Anabel was startled by the number of servants. Seeing her expression, Norbury said, "My mother holds to the formalities of her girlhood. She will laugh about it, but she will not give them up. Come, let us go and see her."

"Shouldn't I go upstairs first?" She put a hand to her hair, wondering if the curls had been crushed by her hat.

"You look lovely." He smiled and took her hand, and Anabel allowed him to lead her up to the spacious drawing room on the first floor.

At first glance, it seemed remarkably full of people. Two sofas were occupied, and a number of gentlemen were leaning against the mantelpiece or turning the pages of newspapers. Anabel hesitated. Norbury squeezed her hand reassuringly, then guided her in, a hand on her elbow. They stopped before an imposing woman, clad in dark green, on one of the sofas, and he said, "Mama, this is Anabel. My mother."

"How do you do?" said Anabel, smiling and giving a sketch of a curtsy.

"My dear." It was plain where Sir Charles got his dark hair and pale green eyes. Indeed, he resembled his mother

in most particulars. She, too, was tall and had a command-
ing presence, and although an ebony cane was propped on
the cushion beside her, she sat very straight. But Anabel
found her gaze cold, and it was not clear whether she was
responding to her greeting or addressing her son.

"How are you feeling?" inquired the latter.

Lady Norbury made a dismissive gesture. "You must
present Lady Wyndham to the others, Charles."

He grimaced slightly, and her stern face relaxed into a
thin smile. "Anabel, this is my Aunt Alice Norbury and
my Aunt Anne Bramton. Uncle Anthony Norbury and
Uncle Gerald Bramton. And these idlers are my younger
cousins. John Norbury." The dark young man lounging
against the mantel raised a negligent hand. "Arthur
Bramton." The pale stripling on the other side of the
fireplace bowed. "And Cecily Bramton." A thin girl on the
sofa opposite stood and curtsied awkwardly. "The older
cousins have better things to do than come down to Kent.
They are all married and parents of hopeful families of
their own." He glanced maliciously at his Uncle Anthony
as he said this, and that gentleman bridled. Anabel realized that that branch of the Norburys was heir to the
property until Charles had children. She looked away.

The older generation seemed indistinguishable at first.
Each murmured a greeting, and Anabel strove to fasten
the correct labels to the faded blond Mrs. Bramton, the
embittered-looking Mrs. Norbury, and the two stout men
who belonged with them. She and Charles sat down, and
silence fell.

"Did you have a pleasant journey?" asked Lady Norbury
after a while.

Anabel waited a moment, but Charles said nothing.
"Yes. It is not far, is it, and the day is so fine."

"Oh, you mustn't say it isn't far," answered young John

Norbury in a jocular tone. "You will spoil Charles' excuse for not coming down more often."

"He comes very often," retorted Lady Norbury crushingly. From the surprised looks the others gave her, Anabel saw that this was a novel pronouncement. "You were a Goring, I believe?" added the hostess.

Anabel glanced at Charles, but he did not seem to find anything amiss with this question. "Yes."

"And you have children?"

"Three," she replied crisply.

"What are their ages?" Lady Norbury seemed wholly unconscious of any rudeness. She might have been asking about the weather.

"William is ten, Nicholas nine, and Susan six." She saw that her tone made the Bramton women wince.

"Ah. Two boys. They are in school, I suppose?"

"No, they are not. They are in London with me because I wished to have them there."

Lady Norbury looked up and met Anabel's eyes. Their gaze held for a moment, and Anabel realized that Charles' mother was by no means as pleased by his engagement as he had told her. In fact, she was not pleased at all. And since Charles had been certain she wished him to marry, it could only be that she did not approve of Anabel. Perhaps a widow with young children was not her idea of a proper bride for her son. Anabel's chin came up defiantly.

"No doubt you are tired after your drive," continued Lady Norbury. "I will have the housekeeper show you your room. I fear I do not get about as I used to. Dinner will be at seven. We keep country hours here. Arthur, will you ring?" He did so, and the silence remained unbroken until the summons was answered. Looking at Charles, Anabel saw that he was unaware of any awkwardness. He had strolled over to the hearth and was exchanging desultory remarks with his cousin John. As she followed the housekeeper from the room she heard Lady Norbury say, "I wish to speak to Charles. We will gather again for dinner." The others were moving toward the door as she left.

Upstairs, in a bedchamber that looked as if it had not been refurbished in a decade, Anabel sat down and thought over her welcome. It was certainly not what she had expected from Charles' glowing reports. His mother was far from the charming, witty creature he had described. She obviously ruled her family with an iron hand, and Charles with some subtler methods. And she disapproved of his choice of a wife. Would she tell him so now? Anabel wondered.

And how did she herself feel about this development? Part of her was annoyed and combative, ready to show Lady Norbury that she had no power over her and that she cared not a whit for her good opinion. Another part wished to go back to London at once and forget the whole matter. Still a third very softly suggested that perhaps her hostess was right.

Pushing this thought aside, Anabel rose to get out her evening dress. It would be a very long visit, she saw. She would speak to Charles and ask him to be more helpful. Once he realized how uncomfortable she felt, he could no doubt do a great deal to ease the situation.

The house party met in the drawing room before dinner. Anabel had changed into a gown of rose pink silk, very severely cut, which she thought should placate Lady Norbury, but when she saw her hostess, forbidding in black satin trimmed with jet, she abandoned that hope. The older members of the family, clearly taking their cue from the hostess, were dour. But John Norbury smiled mischievously at her when she came in, and Arthur Bramton offered her a chair. She took it, wondering where Charles could be and how he could leave her to face this scene alone.

Silence fell. Anabel looked around. The aunts and uncles avoided her eye. Cecily looked frightened. Anabel tried to think of some commonplace remark to begin a conversation, but the atmosphere in the room seemed to press in on her brain, stifling thought.

"I trust you are recovered from your journey," said Lady Norbury at last.

"Yes, thank you."

"One must be more careful, past a certain age, not to wear oneself down."

Anabel's blue eyes widened, then her eyelids dropped. If her hostess thought she would take such gibes, she was mistaken. "Do you find it so?" she answered sweetly. "I myself am never tired."

John Norbury snickered. His formidable aunt silenced him with a glance, then turned back to Anabel with a glare of combined anger and surprise. More than one adversary had mistaken Anabel's fragile looks for timidity in the past. "You have a quick tongue."

"Thank you," answered Anabel perversely.

"You are very pleased with yourself, are you not?" Lady Norbury sounded goaded, and Anabel wondered what Charles had said to her during their tête-à-tête.

"Not overly pleased, I hope." It was very odd, she thought, the way no one else in the room spoke at all. They might have been wax figures. Were they really so firmly under Lady Norbury's thumb?

"Indeed?" The older woman sounded contemptuous.

To Anabel's vast relief, Charles came in. He smiled at her and at his mother, not seeming to see the others, and said, "I'm sorry to be late. My valet is a careless fellow."

The butler, who had been on the watch, announced dinner. Lady Norbury stood slowly and gazed at Charles.

He obediently offered his arm. The aunts and uncles paired up and hurried to follow. Cecily clutched her brother's arm when he would have approached Anabel, which left her to John Norbury.

"What do you think of this bedlam house?" he murmured as they walked toward the dining room.

She merely raised her eyebrows. She would not make the mistake of talking freely to any of these people.

"Right. Mum it is. But I'll give you a piece of advice. If you really want to marry Charles—can't see it myself, but you've accepted him—get him away from here and keep him away until the knot's tied. My aunt is poison."

Anabel looked at him curiously.

"Wondering why the heir apparent is so loose-tongued?" He laughed a little. "*I* don't want this place. I'd as soon live in a mausoleum." They had entered the dining room, and he escorted her to a chair between his father and his uncle before going to his own, farther down the table. Anabel slid into it quickly—the others were already settled, Charles beside his mother—and the meal began.

It was long, slow, and, to Anabel, excruciating. Her neighbors did not speak to her. The only conversation was at the head of the table, and a few murmurs on the opposite side, where the cousins alternated with the aunts. There were five courses, each consisting of far more dishes than she could sample, and the intervals between them seemed endless. At first Anabel was uneasy. She tried more than once to elicit some comment from the uncles. Then she felt inexpressibly weary and bored, and finally angry at the way she was being treated. Why didn't Charles say something? she wondered. But by the time the last course was offered round, her pique had given way to amusement. It was really ridiculous, this solemn party, the heavy silence, the furtive eyes of the people around her. Whatever they might feel, Lady Norbury had no hold on *her*, and she refused to allow her spirits to be depressed. The evening would end eventually, and tomorrow she would depart, never to visit here willingly again. The future implications of this decision she pushed aside.

At last Lady Norbury rose, signaling the ladies' departure. Taking her cane, she walked slowly along the table, spurning an aunt who offered assistance. "Do not linger too long over your port," she told the gentlemen.

"Don't worry, Mama," replied Charles. "We shall join you soon."

The walk upstairs was slow. Everyone kept behind Lady Norbury, and she obviously found the climb very difficult. But she refused help again, sharply, and nothing more was said.

At the drawing-room doorway, Anabel excused herself and ran up another flight. She was determined to stay in her room until it seemed likely that the gentlemen would have come up. She could not face another period of icy silence, or another exchange with Charles' mother.

She calculated correctly. When she entered the drawing room again, the whole party was there. Defiantly she crossed to sit beside Charles on a sofa. He smiled at her and turned back to his mother. The others remained as before.

Anabel watched their interaction curiously. She had not considered it until now, but Charles' devotion to his mother was uncharacteristic. It did not seem to fit his Corinthian pose. She listened to their conversation.

If asked, she would have predicted that Lady Norbury complained about her ills, questioned her son's doings, and tried to dictate to him. She was mistaken. Lady Norbury was hardly talking at all. She was listening to her son repeat some triumph he had achieved—Anabel did not completely understand what; she had missed the beginning of the anecdote—and murmuring praise and admiration as he spoke. When he finished, she added that she had always known he was superior to any man in the country, let alone London, and Charles smiled slightly, as if he acknowledged a truth rather than a compliment.

This went on for half an hour, Anabel growing more and more amazed. She had never heard such a litany of self-congratulation. They did not discuss any other person or any events but those in which he had participated. It was as if the world existed only for Charles to shine in it. She watched his face. He seemed younger. The bored mask was gone, revealing an intense, eager personality that might have been very attractive had his attention ever wandered from himself. Shaken, Anabel rose and walked over to a window, parting the curtains to look out on the moonlit drive. Charles did not seem to notice, though Lady Norbury did. Anabel's mind felt peculiarly blank. She looked out but did not really see anything.

"My mother says Charles was indulged all out of reason," whispered a voice close beside her. Starting, she turned to find John Norbury at her side. "I heard her tell Papa so. My Aunt Norbury has insisted he was perfect since he was born."

Anabel moved away from the window to face the room.

"I suppose we can't talk about that, either. This place makes me nervous as a cat." He paused. "Do you like London?"

"Uh . . . yes, very much."

"*I* haven't been. But I shall, as soon as I come of age." He eyed his parents darkly.

Before Anabel could do more than wonder how to respond to this, Charles was helping his mother to her feet and looking around for her. "Mama retires early," he said. "I shall just take her up. I won't be a moment."

Anabel came forward to say good night. Lady Norbury acknowledged it with a nod, and the two went out.

It was as if a great weight had been lifted from the group. Mrs. Norbury leaned forward to speak to Mrs. Bramton, and the two uncles beat a hasty retreat, muttering about the smoking room. Arthur Bramton joined Anabel and John, and after a hesitant moment Cecily followed. "Whew," Arthur murmured. "That's over. These dinners are almost more than I can stand." Cecily cast a frightened glance at her mother, but the older women were paying no attention.

"How about a game of billiards?" suggested John. "All of us. We can trade off."

"Right." Arthur nodded. "Come, Cecily, I'll give you four strokes." They all looked at Anabel.

"I must wait for Charles."

"He'll come and find us," said John.

She was tempted, but she did not really want to play billiards. She wanted to talk to Norbury. "No, you go on."

John shrugged and led the others out. Anabel returned to the sofa, smiling to show that she would be happy to join in the aunts' conversation. But they were discussing some stranger's prolonged illness, and as they did not explain any of the particulars, she was soon lost.

It seemed hours before Charles reappeared. Lady Norbury had no doubt kept him as long as she could. But finally he came in, smiled at her, and held out a hand. "Come, there is something I want to show you."

She was happy to follow. He led her downstairs to a door opening on the back terrace; they walked across it and onto a gravel path bisecting the lawn. "I should get a shawl," said Anabel.

"It isn't cold. Come."

She took his arm, and they walked to a copse some way from the house. The path twisted among the trees and then emerged in front of a tiny white gazebo, the interior furnished with dark green cushions. Moonlight was pouring over the small clearing in which it sat, gilding everything with silver, and the air was very soft and still. "Come," said Charles again, and he led her up two steps and seated her on a cushion. "This has always been one of my favorite places."

"It is lovely."

He sat beside her and pulled her close within the circle of his arm. "You see? You don't need a shawl." His clasp tightening, he kissed her slowly.

But Anabel was too unsettled to respond. When he drew back, she moved a little away and said, "Charles, I must talk to you about something."

His hand caressed her shoulder. "What?"

"Has . . . has your mother said anything to you about me?"

"She thinks you charming." He started to pull her close again.

"But, Charles." She did not yield. "Did she say so?"

"I can tell what she thinks." He sounded impatient. "She is very happy for me, for us. There is nothing for you to worry over." And as if the issue were settled, he bent his head again, his free hand coming up to encircle her waist and mold her against him. His kiss was insistent and compelling. Anabel found her thoughts becoming less clear. Could she have imagined Lady Norbury's resistance? He must know his own mother better than she, after all. And did it matter?

But as Charles' expert lips and hands once more lulled her into a kind of blank surrender, a remote part of Anabel objected. She stiffened. She was nearly reclining on the cushions by this time, Charles bending over her. She struggled to sit up.

For a moment he prevented her. Then he seemed to recollect himself and drew back. "You are right, my love," he agreed. "We had best go in. This is a dangerous meeting place." He looked around the tiny space as if reviewing fond memories, but he stood, pulling her up against his side and moving toward the door. "We must decide on a wedding date, however, my darling. I am on my best behavior, but I am not superhuman." They walked outside and back along the path. "What about three weeks from tonight? We needn't make too great a fuss. That should give you time to prepare."

"I . . . I must think," she replied breathlessly, conscious of a strong desire to put off this decision.

He chuckled. "I am happy to know that I can so disrupt your thoughts. We will talk it over tomorrow." They had reached the terrace door again. "But tonight, one last farewell." Sweeping her into his arms, he kissed her passionately again.

Chapter Twelve

In London, the following morning dawned bright and clear, but in the schoolroom at Lady Goring's house, storm signals appeared as soon as the children finished their breakfast. "I don't want to do lessons," Susan told her brothers. "I want to go riding first, as we do at home."

"We can't," responded William. "We haven't any horses, and we can't hire them ourselves."

"Why not?" Susan's little face was screwed into a mighty scowl.

"Well . . ." William turned to Nicholas.

"They wouldn't give them to us," the latter said. "And anyway, we wouldn't be allowed to ask. Perhaps Uncle Christopher will take us again soon."

"I hate it here!" declared Susan. "At home I can go riding whenever I like."

Though this was not strictly true, neither of the boys dared point this out to her.

"When is Mama coming home?" she added. "She has been gone forever."

"This afternoon," answered Nick. "She promised to sit with us at our dinner."

"Will she bring that man?"

"No." Then, realizing that he could not guarantee this, Nick amended, "I don't think she will."

"She has been visiting him," replied his sister accusingly.

"His family, yes."

"And when they are married, he will live with us all the time, will he not?"

Nicholas nodded wearily. He recognized Susan's mood. She was at her most intractable, and it was going to be a tiresome day.

"I don't like him!"

"We know that. Neither do we."

The governess came in then, and their conversation was cut off. But throughout the morning lessons Susan glowered, and William and Nicholas waited apprehensively for the explosion that always followed these sulks. After one blast of temper Susan would be all right again, they knew.

It did not come. Instead Susan grew quieter, and when they were dismissed for luncheon, she declared she was not hungry and was going to her room. The boys could only be grateful for her unusual restraint. They discussed it over bread and milk at the nursery table. "I expect she's up to something," said William. "She always is when she gets quiet."

Nick frowned. "But what?"

His brother shrugged, concentrating on his plate.

Before they finished, Nurse came in. "Where is Miss Susan?" she asked them.

"In her room. She said she wasn't hungry."

"She must eat her luncheon. Go and fetch her at once."

"But we're eating," objected Nick, not at all eager to confront his sister.

Nurse put her hands on her hips and glared, and both

boys rose and went along the hall to Susan's room. "I expect she'll let loose now," sighed Nick. William nodded glumly.

Susan's bedchamber was empty, however. There was no sign that she had been there since rising. Exchanging a puzzled look, they went to the schoolroom. It was also untenanted. "Why would she go downstairs?" wondered William.

"Perhaps she changed her mind about eating and went to ask Cook for something special," suggested his brother. They descended to the kitchen, but Susan had not been seen there. Frowning now, they hurriedly looked into the rooms on the other floors. Susan was nowhere in the house.

"I *told* you she was up to something," said William as they paused before her room again. "Where can she have gone?"

Nicholas was thinking hard. "Go and give Nurse some excuse," he said. "We must plan."

"What excuse?" answered William helplessly.

"Think of something!"

Shaking his head, he went, only to return in a moment with the news that Nurse wasn't there. "I think she went down for more milk. The pitcher was gone."

"Good." Nick pulled his brother into Susan's room and shut the door. "We must decide what we are going to do."

"About what?"

"Susan's run away."

"Run . . . ! How do you know?"

"I checked the room while you were gone. She's taken her cloak and the net purse Mama gave her at Christmas. You know she keeps all her pocket money in it. And . . ." He paused for effect. "The cat's gone as well."

William snorted. "He's always gone somewhere."

"No. She's been very careful since he ate the leg of lamb

140

in the kitchen. She made this bed for him and everything." He indicated a nest of old blankets in the corner. "She's gone."

"But . . . where?"

Nick shook his head. "Home, I expect. Remember her complaining this morning?"

"But she can't get home by herself!" William was aghast.

"Try convincing Susan of that."

Silently they thought of their sister's stubbornness. "Mama will be furious," said William. "We must tell someone, start a search."

"Ye-es." Nick was hesitant.

"Of course we must. Come on!" William started toward the door.

"Wait a moment."

He hesitated with one hand on the doorknob.

"I think we should go after her ourselves. That way, no one need know she has run away."

William gaped at him. "Have you run mad? We should never get her back here even if we found her."

"Why not?"

"Because she won't listen to us, bacon brain. She never does."

"I believe I can convince her."

William shook his head and started to turn the knob.

"Are we just to sit in this house, then, as we have been doing for weeks and weeks?" Nick's voice was exasperated. "What's happened to you, William? Have you turned cow-hearted?"

"This isn't one of your pranks, Nicholas! Susan is wandering about London alone. It's not a question of—"

"We could find her. We know how she thinks."

"I don't!"

"Oh, come, William. Let us at least *try*."

The older Wyndham hesitated, obviously torn between

duty and the call of adventure. "I suppose we could look around for an hour or so, then come and fetch help if we had no luck."

"That's the ticket," agreed Nick, ready to accept even partial capitulation.

His brother frowned, then gave in. "Oh, very well." And a few minutes later, having gathered the necessary supplies, the two boys slipped unseen out the front door and into the street.

It was hardly half an hour after that that the bell rang to announce a caller. No footman or maid appeared in the hall, and after a pause the bell rang again. Georgina Goring was hurrying across the upper landing just then, and she hesitated, looking worried, then ran down the stairs and opened the wide front door a bit, peering out through the narrow aperture. "Oh, Mr. Hanford!" She pulled the door wider. "I'm sorry no one came. We are all rather upset. The children have disappeared." Seeing a movement behind him, she drew in her breath. "Susan! Do you have them, then? Thank God!"

Christopher was frowning. "Susan came to see me about an hour ago. Are the boys missing as well?"

"I did not come to see you!" declared Susan irately. "I was running away, and I thought you would help me." She pushed past them and into the hall. "Have William and Nicholas gone, too? If I had known, I would have waited for them."

Christopher exchanged a wry glance with Georgina. "They aren't here," she said. "Nurse discovered it a few minutes ago and fell into a fit of hysterics."

"Nurse did?" responded Susan with ghoulish glee. "She is silly."

Hanford shut the door and went down on one knee beside the little girl. "Susan, where have Nicholas and

William gone? Running away is not going to solve anything. You must see that."

"It would," insisted Susan, "if you would help me. I do not see why you are being so stuffy. Mama can live with that man, and I will live with *you*." She gazed at him with a mixture of appeal and irritation.

His face showed pain for a moment, but he answered merely, "I fear that isn't possible, Susan." Georgina, watching him, bit her lower lip; she thought she had never known anyone so noble. "Now, where have they gone?" asked Hanford again.

"I don't know." She sounded uninterested. "They didn't tell *me* they were leaving. They don't tell me anything."

He took her shoulders and looked into her green eyes. "Is that true? Did you not plan to run away at the same time?"

"No! William mentioned it once, but Nicholas said it was wrong, and he agreed with him. They worry about everything!" She considered the matter. "I suppose they only went because *I* did, and they finally saw what a splendid idea it was."

Christopher stood. "I think she is telling the truth. She does not know where they are."

"What are we going to do?" said Georgina. "Anabel will be so worried."

"I believe I can guess their object."

She gazed at him in admiration. "What?"

"I imagine they have gone after Susan."

"Oh!" Georgina looked at the little girl with amazement.

Susan crowed with laughter. "They have! They have! How stupid boys are."

"I think I can find them," added Hanford, eyeing Susan with amusement and resignation. "I wager they've started for home, thinking that she went there."

"As if I would be so silly," exclaimed the child. "I know

I cannot get so far alone." She glanced at Hanford with annoyance. "I thought *you* would take me."

"I am sorry I could not." He turned to Georgina. "I will leave Susan with you. And I shall hope to return with the boys before the day is out. Tell Anabel."

Georgina nodded. "She should be back at any moment."

His face clouded, remembering where she had gone, then he straightened and nodded. Georgina thought again how splendid he was and wondered how her cousin could reject him for Sir Charles Norbury.

"I am going with you," declared Susan.

"No. You must stay here and see your mother."

"I don't want to see her! I *shall* come. I shall!"

Christopher, impatient to be gone now that he had formed a plan, was unwilling to take the time to cajole her. "Very well. We should be no more than a few hours," he told Georgina. "Susan will be just as well with me. Indeed, she will be less trouble, I imagine. You can tell them where we have gone."

Georgina nodded earnestly.

"Don't worry." He smiled at her. "I'm sure they are all right, and I shall have them back very soon."

"You are so good to do this!" she could not help but say.

He raised his eyebrows. "The children are very dear to me." Susan grasped his hand and pulled it impatiently. "Yes, we are going. We will see you later today, Miss Goring."

"Good-bye."

When she closed the door behind them, Georgina leaned on it, her face dreamy with admiration. Anabel might be older and more experienced than she, but she was still very foolish. Anyone could see that Mr. Hanford was far finer than Sir Charles. If only he . . . but no, he loved Anabel; that was plain. How could she fail to see it? Or did she know? Was she simply letting him love her and

144

enjoying the sensation, while she dallied with Norbury? Georgina frowned. She had seen such behavior here in London and found it shocking. Some members of the *haut ton* lived by a set of rules far removed from those her countrified father had instilled in her. She had not thought that Anabel was one—but Norbury? She frowned in doubt. It would be unbearable if Christopher Hanford were being so grievously hurt on a whim. Even as this idea made her scowl the bell rang again. Georgina started and turned to open the door.

Anabel swept in, looking irritable, followed by Sir Charles and a servant carrying her case. Georgina started to speak.

"My lady!" shrieked Nurse from the upper landing. "Oh, my lady, thank God you are home! The children are gone. They've disappeared!"

Anabel stared up at her in horror.

"They were just as usual when I got them up," she continued. "They had their lessons. But during luncheon I went down for more milk, and when I returned, they were gone. Oh, my lady, do you think they've been kidnapped?"

"Nonsense," drawled Sir Charles. "I daresay they have simply gone to the park or some such thing. Get hold of yourself, woman." He, too, seemed annoyed. Georgina glared at him, and Nurse bridled.

"Have you searched?" asked Anabel in a strangled voice.

"All the men are looking," Nurse replied. "Lady Goring was out, but I have sent after her. I would have gone myself, but—"

"It is all right, Anabel," began Georgina.

"Of course it is," interrupted Norbury. "You are all making a great fuss about nothing. I daresay they will come home directly, very pleased with the uproar they have caused."

"They do not go out alone in London," said Anabel.

She gazed about the hall, distracted. "I must look for them. May I use your carriage?"

"A traveling chaise? You would be much better off—"

"I don't care what sort of carriage it is!"

He stiffened at her tone. "Very well. Of course."

"Anabel," called Georgina, but she was waved aside as they climbed up and urged the driver to start.

Chapter Thirteen

That afternoon was probably the worst of Anabel's life. She had been very glad to return home. Norbury had pressed her all through the journey to set a definite date for their wedding, and she had steadfastly resisted doing so. Some part of her wanted more time for that decision. The exchange had irritated them both. Norbury had been infuriated at this thwarting of his wishes; he was accustomed to capitulation. And Anabel had felt beleaguered. She was still very unused to directing her own life, and the effort of not only taking a position but holding to it in the face of strong opposition exhausted her.

In this mood she had discovered the loss of her children, and nearly fallen into a panic. Questions of her future with Charles evaporated. Never since their birth had she not known where her children were or with whom. The thought of them wandering alone and unprotected in London made her frantic.

Sir Charles offered her no aid. He rode with her as she directed the chaise through the park, oblivious to the stares of fashionable saunterers, and around the streets near the

Goring house. But he sat back in a corner, arms folded, making his disapproval of her actions palpable. At first Anabel didn't notice, but as time passed and they found no clue, she turned to him in desperate need of reassurance. "Can you think of anywhere else we might look?" she asked.

"I think this whole exercise is futile," he replied. "You cannot see anything from a moving carriage. We may have missed them repeatedly in the park. More than likely, they have turned up at home by now, happily unconscious of causing any anxiety."

"Do you truly think so?" She wanted to believe this.

"Yes." He was offended both by her stubbornness on the subject of their wedding and by her complete forgetfulness of him during the last two hours. He was convinced that the children would return, and her exaggerated concern inflamed his jealousy. She had not shown this much emotion for him.

"Perhaps we should go back and see." Anabel was torn. The afternoon was ending, and they hadn't found the children. Yet it was difficult to give up. They might be around the very next corner. She looked at Norbury, whose set face was turned away. He could be right. "Very well. Let us do that."

He gave the order to the driver, and they turned toward home. Unbending a little at her acquiescence to his suggestion, he said, "Have your children any close acquaintances in town? Perhaps they went visiting without telling anyone."

Anabel straightened abruptly. "Christopher! Why didn't I think of him at once?"

Norbury looked displeased.

"We must stop at his sister's house and inquire. It is on the way." Anabel felt revitalized. Christopher would know what to do even if he had not seen the children. The mere thought of him comforted her immensely. How could she have forgotten to consult him? She sat back, relaxing for almost the first time that day.

Norbury's sidelong glance was cold.

But at the Lanforth house they were told that Christopher had gone out of town. He had left so hurriedly that none of the servants had been informed of his purpose, and Amelia had been out all day and thus had not seen Susan or heard of the trouble. She was very sympathetic but could offer no help. Certain that he would return before evening, Hanford had not left her a note.

Unreasonably, Anabel felt deserted and betrayed. She was not thinking clearly and knew only that her mainstay had failed her. She allowed Norbury to direct the carriage home and to help her down when they reached her mother's house, but her mind was full of dreadful visions of what might befall unguarded children in the city streets.

Lady Goring met her at the front door, enfolding her in her arms. "Anabel, my dear. Are you all right?"

"Have they come home?"

"No. But all the servants are out searching. They cannot fail to find them very soon."

Slumping against her mother's shoulder, Anabel burst into tears. Lady Goring embraced her, stroking her hair and murmuring soothing phrases as all the tension and worry of the day poured forth.

Norbury, forgotten, stood stiffly beside the front door. He was not intimidated by female tears. He had seen many in his life. But he was accustomed to being the central figure in such scenes. He could soothe or spurn with equal skill when a woman's feelings for him gave way to sobs; he had had no experience, however, with outbursts from other causes. And he didn't much care for them. The intense emotion that seemed only natural when he himself was the object appeared hysterical and unnecessary here. To him children were rather like dogs. They went their uncharted ways and returned when hungry or weary. He had never felt any great attachment to either species. "My horses will take cold," he said. "Perhaps I should go home and change." Meeting Lady Goring's contemptuous look, he added, "I will return at once, of course, and remain with you until the children return."

Anabel did not surface, but Lady Goring dismissed him with a curt wave that might have offended him if he had not been so eager to depart. When he had gone, Lady Goring helped her daughter up the stairs to the drawing room and removed her bonnet. Her sobs lessened a little. "I will get you some water."

The room was dim. Darkness was falling, and there were no servants in the house to draw the curtains and light the candles. Anabel struggled for control and slowly managed to stop crying. She groped for a handkerchief and wiped her streaming eyes, sniffing.

Georgina rose from an armchair in the corner and approached. She had been sitting here in the dimness for some time, waiting for Anabel's return. Her cousin's crying had touched her deeply, and she had delayed only until it seemed that her news would be understood before rising to impart it. "Anabel," she said.

Anabel started violently and looked up, her eyes red and swollen. "Oh, Georgina. I didn't know you were here."

"I have been waiting to tell you—"

"You might have been out helping us search. But of course my children are not *your* responsibility." At some level Anabel knew this was utterly unfair, but Norbury's abandonment had cut her to the quick, and it seemed to her that no one cared for her or her plight. Christopher was gone, and the man she had agreed to marry was merely annoyed by her anguish. In her upset she turned on the nearest available object.

Georgina understood some of this. "I did not go because—"

"Oh, it doesn't signify," interrupted Anabel bitterly. "Why should you? My promised husband has gone off to change his coat. And my dearest friend has gone out of town without a word. Charles hardly knows the children, of course, and he means to return. But Christopher *might* have done something. How could he be so thoughtless?" This was even more unreasonable, she knew. Christopher could not have known that an emergency would arise. But Anabel was conscious only of a need for his stalwart presence; she was incapable of logical thought.

Georgina was outraged. Not only was the noble, unselfish Mr. Hanford being unjustly accused but Anabel actually dared to praise Sir Charles Norbury at his expense. It was more than unfair; it was intolerable. Georgina's pity for her cousin dissolved in righteous anger. As Lady Goring returned with a tray she threw back her head and strode from the room.

"Oh, dear," sighed Anabel as her mother urged her to try to eat something. "I have offended Georgina. I didn't mean to say such ridiculous things. I don't know what is the matter with me."

"Of course you do. You are terribly upset. Georgina understands that." Anabel was Lady Goring's chief concern just now. She had no doubt Georgina would recover. "Do take just a little of this soup. It will make you feel better."

The evening passed without news. Some of the servants returned, having looked everyplace they could think of, and at nine one of Norbury's footmen arrived with a note saying that he would call in the morning. Lady Goring read this with a curled lip and did not even tell Anabel. She had not asked for Sir Charles and was clearly not thinking about him. Georgina came in a bit later, looking repentant and wanting to speak to Anabel, but Lady Goring insisted she go to bed, refusing to listen to a word. Georgina actually told her the truth, in a rather disjointed sentence, but her aunt's attention was so wholly taken up with her daughter that she did not really hear, merely replying, "Yes, dear, you can tell us all about it tomorrow. Now run along upstairs."

Slowly and reluctantly Georgina went. She felt very uncertain, but she was not accustomed to forcing her opinions on other people, and Lady Goring stood in the place of a parent. She decided to wait in her bedchamber for a while and then try again to tell her story. Unfortunately she had no sooner lain down on her bed to wait than the emotional exhaustions of the day descended, and she fell deeply asleep.

Anabel and her mother remained in the drawing room, with no thought of retiring. Anabel's feelings ran the gamut from guilt and apprehension to sudden, wild hope when a passing carriage seemed to slow before their door. Finally, at eleven, she leaped to her feet, crying, "They have gone home, of course! They dislike London and have often asked to go. I must start out at once."

Lady Goring rose also, frowning. "Do you think so?" She did not really believe that the children would flee without a word.

"Yes, yes. That must be it. Will you order the carriage for me, Mama? I will just fetch my hat and cloak."

"But, Anabel, this does not sound like William or Nicholas. And I do not think they would allow Susan to lead them." Realizing that her daughter had not really heard her, she took her shoulders in a firm grip and met her wildly elated gaze. "Besides, Anabel, you cannot search for them in the darkness. We must wait for morning now."

"No!" She struggled free. "I must do something!"

"I understand how you feel, but it is no good wearing

yourself out tonight. You might easily pass them in the dark."

Abruptly Anabel's eagerness collapsed. "Oh, Mama, what am I going to do?" She dropped onto the sofa again and put her head in her hands. "It is all my fault. I should never have gone away."

"Nonsense. If it comes to that, it is my fault. They were lost from my house. But we won't waste time repining. First thing tomorrow, we shall begin an organized search. We can have the Bow Street runners."

Her daughter looked up, "We will find them, won't we?"

"Of course! There is no question about that."

Trying to smile, Anabel held out her hand. Lady Goring took it and squeezed it reassuringly, hoping that she was indeed right. "Why not go up to bed?" she urged finally. "Nothing can be done just now."

"I couldn't sleep. You go on."

"No. I shall stay with you."

They lapsed into silence again. Midnight passed, and the sounds from the street outside gradually subsided. The ticking of the mantel clock became loud. Anabel seemed to feel it inside her head.

At last both women began to droop. Such a high pitch of anxiety could not be sustained indefinitely. Lady Goring's head gradually dropped onto the back of the armchair, and she dozed. Anabel, though she didn't sleep, curled into the corner of the sofa in a kind of stupor. Thus, when they heard the sound of carriage wheels approaching the house in the small hours of the morning, they both started up convulsively, jarred by the sudden noise in the predawn silence.

"It is nothing," said Anabel shakily, sinking back. "A carriage." But she strained to listen.

"It is slowing." Her mother went to the window. "I

think . . . yes, it is stopping here, Anabel." The other was already at the drawing-room door, then running for the stairs.

They had the front door open before the vehicle was completely stopped. Anabel found it difficult to breathe as it pulled up and the door swung open. But when first William, then Nicholas emerged, she rushed forward and swept them into her arms, shaking with joy and relief.

The boys were sleepy. They accepted their mother's embraces in good part, but they also bore her backward toward the house and their beds. "Where have you been? Where did you go? Where is . . ." Anabel looked up at this moment and saw before her Christopher Hanford, cradling a drowsy Susan in his arms. She was struck speechless.

"Everyone come inside," ordered Lady Goring. She herded the boys before her and put a hand in the small of Anabel's back. They all went in and upstairs to the drawing room once more.

"I'm tired," complained William, stretching and yawning.

Lady Goring looked from Anabel to Hanford. "I will take you up to bed," she answered. "Here, Mr. Hanford, give me Susan."

"I will take her if you like."

"Nonsense. She is quite light. I can manage." Urging the boys before her again, she went out.

Silence fell. Anabel stared at Christopher as if she had never seen him before, and he waited, uncertain. Then, as if impelled by some external force, she ran forward and threw herself into his arms, burying her face in his shoulder.

Hanford was startled for a moment. In all the years they had known each other, he and Anabel had never embraced. Moreover, he could not understand her violent reaction to their return. He had left a clear message of his intentions. But these concerns were soon lost in sensation. For the first time Christopher held the woman he had loved for so long. Against hope, she had come to him. Throwing questions to the wind, he tightened his arms around her and, when she looked up, bent to fasten his lips passionately on hers.

Anabel was beyond surprise. When she had seen Christopher holding Susan, it had felt as if a lightning bolt went through her brain, dazzling her senses and paralyzing thought. She knew only that something had happened to her; she could not interpret it. Moving into Christopher's arms had seemed natural, and when she rested her head on his shoulder, she suddenly felt as if everything were all right again, after an endless agony. She had raised her head to say something like this, only to be overtaken by his kiss.

This was equally astonishing. She had never thought of kissing Christopher, but now his touch seemed to set her on fire. She had never felt anything like it. Her hands moved of their own volition to caress his upper arms, his shoulders, and to tighten about his neck. She felt his lean strength along the length of her body and was acutely aware of every contact. She felt no languor, as she had with Norbury; every part of her seemed newly alive and singing with energy.

At last, reluctantly, Hanford drew back. He had felt Anabel's response, and it had filled him with joy and redoubled ardor. But, inevitably, other concerns intruded. He could not wholly forget that she was promised to another man.

Anabel took two trembling breaths and moved away. She could not assimilate this change quickly after the day she had had. Her familiar world had turned upside down. "I . . ." She swallowed. "Where did you find them?"

"On the road home, as I suspected. They were indignant when they saw that Susan was with me."

"With you?" Anabel thought that perhaps her brain was not working properly. His words made no sense to her.

"Yes." He frowned. "Didn't Georgina tell you?"

"Georgina?" She was completely lost.

"She promised to . . . never mind. Susan came to my sister's house this afternoon . . . or yesterday it is now. She informed me that she was running away and I was to help her." He smiled slightly. "Naturally I brought her back, but by the time we arrived the boys had already departed in search of their sister. They concluded that she was going home and took that road. I guessed and followed in my traveling carriage, coming up with them some hours later." He shook his head. "They were very resourceful; they had convinced a carter to give them a ride. Susan insisted upon coming along when I would have left her here. But I told Georgina my plan." He stepped forward and took her icy hands in his warm ones. "Didn't she tell you?"

"No!" Anabel considered. "That is, she may have tried. I was very worried."

"Poor Anabel." He made as if to embrace her again, but she drew away.

"I . . . thank you!"

He shrugged, dismissing her thanks, and waited. He would not force her into any declaration, but neither was he willing to help her avoid the issue. Her response to him had been unmistakable; she would have to say something.

For her part, Anabel did not know what to do. A great many things were coming clear to her, and others clamored for her attention. It was obvious that she had made a complete mull of things so far. She did not want to compound her mistakes. But when she looked into Christopher's eyes, she could think of nothing but him. "I . . . I'm exhausted," she said, gazing at the floor. "And I must see that the children are all right. Will you . . . will you come to call tomorrow, so that I may thank you properly?"

What did she mean by "properly"? he wondered. But he could only agree. She did look tired. "Of course." He hesitated, hoping she would speak again, then turned and went slowly out. Anabel collapsed on the sofa and sat very still, listening to the front door open and shut and the sound of his carriage driving away.

Chapter Fourteen

She didn't go up to the children. She remained where she was, her body motionless but her mind racing. Everything that had happened to her in the last three months had suddenly taken on a new significance. It was as if with one small shift in her outlook, all those events had changed, so that she had to review each one and alter her ideas about it. Christopher had been the center of her life for some time, she saw now; it was only when he had left to go abroad that she had felt restless at home. Her feelings for him had been growing deeper and stronger for years. Why she had not seen it before she did not know. Perhaps the easy gradualness of the process had disguised it. They had been so in harmony and so content with each other that she had never before had occasion to draw back and examine the situation. She had taken him wholly for granted, not pausing to think how fortunate she was to have him always near.

And when he had gone, she was hurt and lonely, she saw now. But she had hidden the knowledge from herself and come up to London, like a fool. She had been no better than a green schoolgirl, awed by new sights and swept into a mistaken engagement. Sir Charles had dazzled her, but he had never touched her heart as Christopher did. Anabel bowed her head on the sofa arm and sighed. How could she have been so stupid? She had thought Sir Charles exciting; he had appealed to her vanity and her pride. But Christopher's kiss tonight had shown her the emptiness of that attraction. Christopher's touch had set her afire with longing; Charles merely induced surrender.

Anabel rose and walked about the room, frowning. She did not even see her mother look in at the door, watch her face for a moment, and then retreat. She was trying to understand her failure and to sort out her feelings so that she could think what to do.

The night was almost over. Outside, the sky was lightening with the first pale hues of dawn, and muted sounds from below indicated that the servants were stirring. But Anabel was aware of nothing but her own inner turmoil. Though exhausted by the emotions of the past day, she did not think of sleep.

When the sun had appeared over the horizon and the scent of breakfast was rising from the kitchen, she was suddenly distracted by the sound of running footsteps on the stairs, and in the next moment Georgina hurtled into the drawing room, still wearing the gown of the night before and looking wild-eyed and crumpled. "Oh, Anabel," she gasped. "I fell asleep. I meant to come back down in a few minutes and speak to you. I do beg your pardon. I was to tell you—"

"I know," she replied. "Christopher told me when he brought back the children."

"He *did*, then? I mean, of course I knew he would, but I wasn't certain when they would arrive."

Anabel merely nodded. She still felt far away.

"Mr. Hanford is wonderful!" exclaimed the girl. "He

knew at once where they had gone, and I suppose he found them without the least trouble. How I wish I had been here when he came back."

Anabel looked at her, and she flushed, then raised her chin. "You admire him very much, don't you?" said Anabel.

"Yes." Georgina sounded defiant.

"Why did you not tell me at once what he was doing?"

"I tried! But no one would listen. And when you began abusing him, I . . ."

She trailed off, feeling guiltily conscious that she had no real excuse.

"Abusing Christopher? I?"

"Well, you were saying that he didn't care, and ranking him below Si—" She stopped herself before saying Norbury's name.

Anabel didn't recall her words, but she had no doubt Georgina was right. "Oh, Georgina—I was very worried. I didn't mean what I said."

"No." Georgina hung her head. "I know. I . . . I beg your pardon, Anabel. I was very stupid."

Her cousin sighed, gazing at the fireplace. "Not so much as I," she murmured.

"What?"

"Never mind, Georgina. It doesn't matter now. The children are safe, and all is well." At least with them, she added to herself.

Georgina eyed her, sensing a difference. "Did you sleep at all?"

"No, I couldn't."

"You should go up now and rest this morning."

Anabel shook her head; she was far too restless still. "The day is beginning. I can sleep tonight. Why don't we go down and have some breakfast? I believe it is ready." She suddenly realized that she was extremely hungry. "Did you have any dinner last night?"

"I . . . no." Georgina seemed surprised.

"Well, then." With an attempt at a smile, Anabel linked her arm with her cousin's.

"Should we change first?" asked the girl, looking from her own crumpled gown to Anabel's creased traveling dress.

"We can do so when we have eaten," declared the other, urging her forward, and they walked down to the breakfast parlor together.

Lady Goring found them there twenty minutes later, surrounded by the remains of a substantial breakfast. "Oh, Mama," said Anabel. "Did the children fall asleep at once? I must go up to them. I would have come last night, but . . ." She hesitated.

"They were asleep almost before I put them to bed, and they are still sleeping now. I asked Nurse on my way down." She looked from one to the other. "What of you?"

"I fell asleep in my gown," replied Georgina sheepishly. She rose. "I must go and change it."

Lady Goring looked at her daughter as Georgina went out. "And you, Anabel?"

"I had too much to think about."

"Indeed?" She surveyed her closely.

"Yes."

She did not explain, and Lady Goring did not press her, despite her curiosity about what had passed between her daughter and Hanford the previous night. It was obvious that *something* had, but she decided it would be best to wait and let it develop.

"I must change also," added Anabel, pushing back her chair. "I will look in on the children when I am dressed."

Lady Goring nodded and reached for the teapot.

But as Anabel was ascending the stairs the bell rang and a footman went to the door. She lingered on the landing, wondering if it could be Christopher so early. But the voice that drifted up to her was that of Sir Charles Norbury, calm and confident of his welcome. He had stepped inside and seen her before Anabel could move. "Ah. There you are," he added, striding quickly up to her. He glanced at her dress. "Are the children not back, then?"

"Yes. They are here." Her lips felt strange, almost stiff.

"As I foretold," he responded, taking her arm and guiding her into the drawing room. "I was right, you see."

This was too much. "My friend Christopher Hanford *brought* them back," she retorted, "after searching for them for most of the night!"

"Indeed?" Norbury's chiseled mouth turned down. "How very, er, enterprising of him. What led him to take this task upon himself?"

"*He* was worried about the children!" As you were not, her tone implied.

"The children, of course," he sneered. "How very touching."

Anabel gazed at him with new eyes. Had Norbury been sympathetic and understanding this morning, as he had not last night, her new viewpoint might have wavered. As it was, she wondered how she could have ever thought she wanted to marry him. Gazing at his fawn pantaloons, his superbly tailored blue coat, and his gleaming Hessians, worn with such assurance and so perfectly complementing his dark, hawklike face, she admitted to herself that his appearance certainly encouraged infatuation. Indeed, he had a power of personality that could overwhelm others' wills. But now that she had discovered her true feelings about Christopher, Norbury's spell was broken, and she knew she would not fall under it again.

Norbury noted the unaccustomed disapproval in her eyes. He was furious at this latest development. Not only had the children's ridiculous prank diverted Anabel from subjects infinitely more important, but now this Hanford was pushing himself forward and trying to ingratiate himself at Norbury's expense. Sir Charles was fully aware of Christopher's feelings for Anabel; the rivalry had added spice to his triumph, and Anabel's ignorance of the contest had been quite amusing. But he sensed a change now. He could not have pointed to the evidence, but a new tone in her voice told him that her opinion of Hanford, and of himself, was altered. Cooler-headed, Norbury might have been conciliating, might even have pretended to admire Hanford's initiative in finding the children, and thus have won back some of Anabel's sympathy. But he was impatient and frustrated by her refusal to plan for the future. He had determined to marry—he wanted to marry—why was she thwarting him?

"I am surprised that the heroic Mr. Hanford is not here," he said contemptuously. "I should have expected him to dig in at the scene of his rescue."

Anabel had her lips pressed very tightly together. She was afraid to answer him for fear of what she might say; she knew it would be disjointed and overemotional. She needed to think carefully and prepare herself to confront him; he was certain to argue, and Anabel hated disputes. "The children are safe, that is all that matters," she answered. "Thank you for calling to inquire about them."

"Of course." He paused. "Shall we sit down?"

"I was just on my way upstairs." She indicated her crumpled gown with a gesture.

"I shan't stay long."

With a sigh, she sat. She was too tired to fight him just now.

"As your worry over the children is so happily set to rest," he continued, "perhaps we might return to another subject—that of our wedding date."

"And a much more important one?" she replied caustically.

"I did not say so." He raised one dark brow.

"Your tone implied it."

"Nonsense. You are imagining things. Now, I looked over the calendar last night, and I have chosen three days that would be suitable." He took a slip of paper from his coat pocket and held it out to her.

Anabel was furious. While she had been sleepless, terrified about her children, Charles had been studying calendars! She did not take the paper. "I have not slept all night," she said, rising. "I am exhausted. We can talk of this another time."

"Surely you can spare a moment." He rose to face her. "You seem remarkably uninterested in this subject. I should think it would be foremost in your mind."

Anabel opened her mouth to tell him that she would never marry him, but a great wave of fatigue engulfed her. It was all too much. She could not form a rational sentence. She shook her head.

Gazing at her, Norbury was forced to admit that she did look worn. Her pallor and drooping posture touched that emotion that had led him to offer for her in the beginning. In his way, he loved her, though this had not taught him to put others' concerns before his own gratification. Slowly he returned the paper to his pocket. "I suppose we can talk tomorrow. One more day will make little difference. You should go to bed."

Anabel merely nodded, grateful to be spared more reproaches.

"I will call in the morning again, and we can settle everything."

Yes, thought Anabel, that will be best. I will prepare myself and tell him then. She nodded again.

Norbury summoned a smile and came toward her. When his arms slipped around her, Anabel did not protest. She could not find the energy. He pulled her close and kissed her gently. Anabel tested her sensations; she felt nothing, not even that boneless surrender he had once evoked in her.

He sensed some change and tightened his hold, kissing her again, more passionately. Anabel remained passive for a moment, then drew back. She did not exactly push him away, but the effect was the same.

"What is the matter?" he demanded, touched on one of his vainest points.

"Nothing. I am tired."

"Indeed?" Her reaction made him angry again. Did she not realize that he had treated her with more consideration than he had any other woman in his history? He had suppressed his passions ruthlessly, and now she begrudged him even a kiss. He felt like shaking her or pushing her to the sofa and showing her precisely what she was rejecting. He was confident of his ability to change her stiffness to eager response.

The image pleased him, and he smiled a little, thinking of the future. If she remained so cool, it would be an even greater pleasure to subdue her. He imagined Anabel pleading for his caresses, and his smile widened.

She did not like his expression. Moving out of his arms, she walked toward the door. "I'm . . . I'm sorry. I am very tired," she repeated.

"Of course. I will take my leave." Following, he took her hand and held it lingeringly to his lips, his pale green eyes holding hers. Then he turned and left the room.

Anabel took a long breath, relieved. What had that strange look in his eyes meant? She had never seen it there before. Sighing, she rubbed her face. She *was* exhausted. Perhaps she should try to sleep after all. She moved toward the staircase and then paused, surprised to hear male voices from downstairs.

"Ah. The conquering hero," said Norbury in a scathing tone.

"Sir Charles." Anabel started. It was Christopher's voice.

"Come to enjoy Anabel's gratitude?" Norbury laughed a little. "It is something, I suppose, though I myself prefer more palpable pleasures." His voice implied a great deal. Anabel flushed.

"I have no doubt of it," answered Hanford, angry but controlled.

"I fear you will find the lady rather tired. In fact, I do not believe she is receiving callers."

"Then I am sure she will tell me so," answered Christopher. "As she has anytime these ten years."

"Ah, yes. You are an *old* friend. Your *comfortable* relationship is admirable. Anabel hardly thinks of you as a man, I believe." This was a clear insult, and Anabel could imagine Norbury's sardonic expression. She stepped forward to intervene.

"You know very little of what Anabel thinks," responded Christopher positively. He spoke without rancor, as if simply stating a truth, but the implications were as cutting as Norbury's. "And now, if you will pardon me. I do not wish to detain you."

There was a slight sound from the staircase, as if one man had jostled the other, a scuffle, then silence. Anabel hurried onto the landing, her heart pounding.

They were facing each other halfway down the staircase, Christopher one step above. Their chests rose and fell rapidly, and both were glaring.

"Christopher!" said Anabel.

The tension broke. Norbury, though he looked furious, bowed very slightly and continued on his way. Hanford ran lightly up to her, a smile replacing his scowl. He had waited for this moment all night, anxious to see how she would receive him. "How are you? Is all well?"

She led him into the drawing room, hearing the door

close behind Norbury as they sat down. "Yes. The children are still asleep after their adventure."

"As you should be." He was scanning her face. "You *are* tired."

"Only a little." It was true that now Christopher was here, she felt much less exhausted.

Their eyes met and held. They did not notice the lengthening silence. Each saw everything he needed to know, and Christopher's hand moved irresistibly to take hers. "Anabel," he murmured at last.

She looked down. How could she have dreamed of preferring Sir Charles to Christopher? she wondered. It seemed so obvious to her now that she had been in love with Christopher for years. And Norbury's polished elegance faded into insignificance beside his warm appeal. She looked sidelong at his ruddy hair and startlingly blue eyes, at the set of his shoulders in his blue coat and the curve of his leg in his yellow pantaloons. Everything about him spoke to her as Norbury could not, never had. Why had she not seen it? How could she have been so foolish?

"I cannot help but speak," said Christopher. "I vowed I would not, unless I had some sign from you. I love you, Anabel, with all my heart and soul."

She took a trembling breath.

"I know you are promised to Norbury." He waited, hoping she would interrupt. "I had thought . . . you have only to say one word, and I will be silent forever on this subject." He bent to see her face. "Do you say it, Anabel?"

"No." She struggled to speak more clearly. "I have made a dreadful mistake, Christopher. I . . . I don't know how I could have been so blind. I love you—I have for the *longest* time."

His heart pounding with elation, Hanford swept her into his arms. Again Anabel felt that leap of response and marveled at the difference. It was some time before they spoke again.

At last they drew apart and smiled tenderly at each other. Christopher settled Anabel's head against his shoulder. "What are you going to do?"

"Break off the engagement. I would have today, but I was so tired. Tomorrow I will speak to him."

He nodded. "I had almost despaired of being so happy."

"I am sorry, Christopher. I—"

He put a hand gently over her mouth, shaking his head. "We won't talk of that. It is over now."

She nodded, and he took his hand away. "I want to go home very soon. Are you ready to leave London?"

"Utterly. We can be married in our own parish church. Vicar Prentice will be delirious with joy."

Anabel turned to him, smiling. "Is that an offer, Mr. Hanford?"

He looked surprised. "Hadn't I offered already?"

"You had not."

"Good God!" Disentangling himself, he sank to one knee before her. "Anabel, would you do me the great honor of becoming my wife?"

She put a hand to her breast and opened her eyes very wide. "Mr. Hanford! I don't know what to say to you."

"The deuce you don't!" He rose and pulled her close again, speaking with his lips brushing hers. "Say yes."

"Yes," she murmured, and he kissed her slowly. Anabel drew her hands along his upper arms to his shoulders, filled with a great happiness. This was the way she should feel, she now knew, every fiber rejoicing in her love's touch. After long searching, she had finally discovered that truth.

Chapter Fifteen

When Christopher had gone, promising to return for dinner that evening, Anabel went upstairs to her bedchamber. She no longer felt like sleeping, and she bathed and put on a primrose sprig muslin gown with fluttering green ribbons. She wanted to sing as her maid brushed out her soft brown hair and dressed it in ringlets around her face. When she was dressed, she walked up to the schoolroom floor, listening for sounds of the children. They were up; she heard them in the nursery and turned that way, opening the door to find them at breakfast. William and Nicholas were eating with great concentration; Susan was slipping a forbidden treat to Daisy, who crouched on the floor beside her feet. They all, except Daisy, who was merely avid, looked happy. Anabel smiled, then sobered and walked into the room to stand over them, crossing her arms on her breast. Nurse, seeing her pose, retreated into the next room.

William grimaced and put down his spoon. Nicholas, becoming aware of her presence late, froze, his spoon poised over his bowl. Susan looked up blithely. "Hello, Mama. Would you like some porridge?"

It taxed all Anabel's faculties not to laugh. She was feeling so happy that she could scarcely bear to scold the children. But they had been very naughty. "No, thank you, Susan," she replied, keeping her voice and expression stern. "I wish to talk to all of you."

The boys cringed.

"You know you have behaved very badly, and you will have to be punished."

"I only went to see Uncle Christopher," protested Susan. "We often do so at *home*." She sounded accusatory.

"Not alone. And not without telling me where you are going," answered Anabel. "And London is not home. You cannot wander about here as you can in our park."

"I *know*," replied the little girl with great feeling.

Anabel's lips twitched, and Nicholas saw it. "We are very sorry, Mama," he said at once. "We will never do it again. We just thought we could find Susan before anyone noticed and bring her back." He made a face at his sister. "We might have known we couldn't think as *she* does."

"No one *asked* you to look for me," retorted Susan. "I was perfectly fine."

"It does not matter what you thought," interrupted Anabel. "You all were at fault, and you all knew you were being naughty. For the next week you will have lessons in the afternoon as well as in the morning, and at the end of that time I will hear you recite what you have learned."

The children groaned. Even Nicholas, who loved books, was not overfond of lessons.

"You will go out only when accompanied by Miss Tate, for a walk in the park."

"But Uncle Christopher promised to take us riding again," protested William.

Anabel thrilled at the name, but she said, "I think you have caused enough trouble for Christopher. What if he had not come after you?"

"We would be home by now," muttered William, then subsided under his mother's frown.

"I want you to understand how serious the results of your misbehavior might have been," she concluded. "You were very fortunate; you could have been hurt or lost. London is very large, and not all parts are safe. Do you see what I mean?"

Slowly William nodded. Nicholas was quick to do so. Susan pouted for a moment. "I knew exactly where Uncle Christopher's house was. I asked him before." Under her mother's eye, she scowled, then shrugged. "I'm sorry."

Anabel smiled. "Good. That is settled, then. And I may give you some good news." All three looked up. "We are going home soon, perhaps in two weeks."

Their faces brightened. "Truly, Mama?" said William.

"Truly. I think we have been in town long enough."

"Hurrah!" replied William, leaping up.

"Did you hear that, Daisy?" said Susan, bending down. "We are going home. You will like it there."

But Nicholas was thoughtful. "Is that man coming with us? Norbury?"

"No." Anabel hesitated. She shouldn't say anything until all was settled, but she couldn't resist. "We won't be seeing him anymore."

"Aren't you going to marry him?" asked Nick.

"No."

"But you said you were."

"I . . . changed my mind." Anabel felt slightly awkward.

"Hurrah!" shouted William again, jerking the back of his brother's chair until he nearly dumped him on the floor. "Everything will be as it was again."

Anabel debated whether to tell them about Christopher, but decided she should wait until she had spoken to Norbury. They would tell the children together, with no fear this time of complaints.

Nick and Susan had risen now, and the three of them were dancing around the room in a ring. Daisy, excited by this movement, streaked in and out between their feet, his claws scrabbling on the wooden floor. In one pass he managed to trip up both William and Nicholas, and the group collapsed in a confused heap, panting. Anabel laughed down at them, and they all grinned. "You had best finish your breakfast," she said. "I expect Miss Tate is waiting for you in the schoolroom."

There was another general groan, but they untangled themselves and returned to the table. "I will see you at dinner," finished Anabel, turning to go. "Uncle Christopher is coming, so you will dine downstairs with us." She shut the door to a general cheer.

"You see?" said Nick complacently when they were alone again. "I told you it would work." He took a large bite of porridge.

"What?" William, too, concentrated on his breakfast again.

"My plan, of course." The others stared at him. "Well, we are going home, are we not? And Mama is not to marry that Norbury."

"Yes, but your plan had nothing to do with it," answered his brother.

"What do you mean?"

"It's all because I ran away," said Susan, her small face smug. "You were too cowardly, but I knew Mama would listen then."

William snorted in disgust. "You are both ninnyhammers. It had nothing to do with either of you." He ignored the clamor of protest this brought down upon him and ate his breakfast.

"If you know so much," said Nick finally, "what did make Mama change her mind?"

William pondered, his spoon vertical in his fist. "I don't know *that*."

The others made derisive noises.

"But I do know that Mama was different today."

"Different?" echoed Susan.

"Yes. Something has happened. You could tell. I don't know what, but that is the reason we are going home, and I don't believe it had anything to do with us."

"Stuff!" replied Susan, bending to offer Daisy a bit of bread. But Nick looked thoughtful.

The day passed quietly for the Goring household, seeming shorter because of the late start. Anabel stayed at home, sitting in the drawing room and pretending to write letters. She actually spent most of the afternoon simply rehearsing the events of the past few weeks and marveling over the outcome. Occasionally she worried about what she would say to Norbury, but since she did not have to face him until the morning, she usually put such thoughts aside. Christopher was much more often in her mind, and at these times a dreamy smile played about her mouth and she forgot everything but memories of what had passed between them.

Lady Goring and Georgina went out shopping late in the afternoon, returning only in time to change for their early dinner. Though Anabel had said nothing to her, Lady Goring was certain that there had been important developments. And the fact that Christopher Hanford was coming to dinner encouraged her greatly. She did not broach the subject, however, fearing to say something wrong and mar the delicate equilibrium she sensed. Mr. Hanford could be trusted to arrange things, she felt. She had been further impressed by his strength of character in the last few days.

Georgina was the first down that evening. She had changed quickly to escape the chatter of her maid, which was all of Mr. Hanford's heroism. Her emotions had been unsettled all day, since she had seen the serene happiness on Anabel's face, so unlike her previous hectic gaiety. Something had happened, she was certain, and it had made her own blunder last night insignificant. But she did not know what, and the mystery made her restless.

She knew that Christopher would never care for her. She had accepted it. But his fate was still very important to her; she thought of him a great deal of the time.

A movement caught her eye, and she started. She had been pacing the drawing-room carpet as she thought, and it was her own reflection in the glass that had attracted her attention. Moving closer, she surveyed it. This was not the Georgina Goring who had come to London. Her father would hardly recognize her. She had shed all of her plumpness by this time; the gray eyes that looked into the mirror seemed large, with unaccustomed depths. In her modish pink gown, with her blond hair dressed à la Diane by Lady Goring's maid, she seemed wholly changed. And it was only right, she thought, for she felt a completely different person, too. So much had happened to her since she came reluctantly up to town.

"Good evening, Miss Goring," said a male voice from the door.

She whirled to find Hanford there, smiling at her. "G-good evening," she stammered past a lump in her throat.

"You're looking very smart." He came forward, gestured toward the sofa, and they sat down.

"Th-thank you."

"I hope you have recovered from the alarms of last night?"

She nodded, then blurted out, "I am so sorry I didn't tell Anabel. I *tried*, but no one would listen to me. And then I fell asleep." She hung her head. This wasn't the strict truth, but she was not going to mention Anabel's criticisms of him.

"It doesn't matter. Things turned out well in the end." And I am grateful you did not speak, he added to himself. If Anabel had known the truth all along, she would not have been quite so happy to see me, and we might never have reached an understanding.

Watching his face, Georgina said, "Did they?" in a tentative voice.

Hanford met her eyes. He had done his best to be kind to this girl while showing her that his affections were firmly engaged elsewhere. He knew that her youthful infatuation with him was nothing more than that; it would fade soon. But he also remembered the painful throes of calf love. He felt no guilt, but there was pity in his gaze as he answered, "Very well. Anabel and I are going to be married, Miss Goring."

"Oh!" Georgina blinked. She had not expected anything so revolutionary. "What about Sir Charles? I mean . . ."

"That is at an end."

"Oh, good," responded the girl before she could think. She flushed bright red. "Er . . . that is . . ."

Hanford laughed. "*I* certainly think so."

"I never liked him somehow," confided Georgina.

"Neither did I," he replied feelingly.

They laughed together. "I wish you very happy. I know that you . . . I noticed . . ." She faltered. Christopher's confidences had made her feel very grown up; yet she didn't know what to say to him. Her own confused feelings seemed to tie up her tongue. She was glad for them. Mr. Hanford had received his heart's desire, and Anabel would be much happier with him than with Norbury. But she also felt a lingering, wistful love for him herself. If it had been she he offered for . . . She thrust this thought aside. There had been no question of that.

"You are a remarkable girl, Miss Goring," added Christopher.

Looking up, she saw in his eyes knowledge of her feelings, and flushed again.

"You have true greatness of spirit, and someday you will be as happy as I am just now." He smiled, hoping to reduce her confusion.

Georgina couldn't think what to say.

"Your first season has been remarkably eventful so far," he continued in a lighter tone. "I wonder if you expected London to be so busy."

"I didn't." Taking his cue, Georgina spoke jokingly. "Indeed, I never imagined half the things I have done."

"I hope you have been enjoying yourself."

"Oh, yes."

They both turned as a footman came in. He held a silver salver on which reposed a folded sheet of paper. "A note for you, Miss Georgina," he said. "The man is waiting for an answer."

"For me?" She tore it open. "Oh, Lydia Mainwaring is holding a waltzing party tomorrow and particularly wishes me to come. I must write her at once." She started out of the room, then remembered Hanford. "If you will excuse me a moment?" Her gray eyes were glowing.

"Of course. I shall be quite all right."

With a smile, Georgina went out. Hanford sat gazing at the opposite wall, a thoughtful smile on his face as well. Georgina would soon forget him, it was clear.

"Mr. Hanford." Lady Goring came in, and he rose to greet her. "How glad I am to find you here alone. I wanted to speak to you."

He raised inquiring eyebrows.

"*What* has happened? I dare not ask Anabel, for fear of spoiling things, but I am agog with curiosity!"

He laughed. "What makes you think something has happened?"

She looked at him, and he laughed again. "If Anabel has not told you—"

"I believe I shall scream with vexation," interrupted Lady Goring.

He relented. "We are going to be married."

She clasped her hands before her. "Truly? And Norbury?"

"Anabel is to tell him tomorrow. I imagine that is why she didn't mention it. She wished to speak to him first."

"Oh, I have never been so glad about anything. Does your sister know?"

Hanford looked surprised. "No. I was waiting until all was settled."

"May *I* tell her?"

He stared at her.

"We have conspired together to match you and Anabel," she explained, "and though our efforts came to nothing, I know her interest in the matter."

He smiled. "I suppose you may. But . . ."

"Oh, I will be discreet. I will call on her tomorrow morning. My dear Mr. Hanford, or Christopher, as I shall call you now, how pleased I am!" She held out her hands and gave his a firm squeeze. "You will both be very happy."

"I believe we will," he answered, returning her glowing look.

Georgina came back, followed closely by Anabel and the children. The latter threw themselves upon Christopher at once, effectively ending conversation, and it was not until they were going into the dining room that he was able to speak privately to Anabel. "How are you?"

"Splendid." They smiled into each other's eyes.

"You haven't told the children?"

"Not yet. I thought we would do that together."

He nodded, pleased. "Tonight?"

"I think tomorrow afternoon would be better. By then everything will be . . ." She gestured.

"Yes. I will call then. I hope they will be pleased."

"Can you doubt it?" They watched the children climbing into their seats at the table. "They will be delighted. Almost as happy as when I told them we are going home soon."

"It will be good to be back."

"Very!" They smiled at each other again. Anabel started to move away toward her chair.

"Oh, Anabel?"

"Yes."

"I'm afraid I wasn't able to resist telling your mother the news when she asked."

"Mama? Why didn't she ask me? I wonder."

His eyes danced. "I believe she was afraid to."

"Afraid?" Anabel giggled.

"I told Miss Goring also. She, ah . . ."

"I know. You have been very kind to her. There were moments when I found it quite annoying."

"If I had only known!"

Anabel laughed again. She felt like laughing all the time now.

"I'm hungry!" declared Susan from the other side of the room. Anabel and Christopher exchanged a last amused glance and went to their places.

It was a lively, hilarious meal. The children were in high spirits, anticipating what they would do when they were home again and wondering about all their friends there, human and animal. They pelted Christopher with questions he could not answer, as he, too, had been away for some time, and formed all sorts of plans for the future. They addressed an equal number of remarks to Anabel, their strategy of silence abandoned. Even Georgina and Lady Goring were urged to come down and be introduced to Susan's remarkable pony and William's amazingly intelligent spaniel. "Daisy is very happy, too," said Susan. "She can't wait to see the country. I have told her all about it."

"That is one of the blessings of this affair," replied Lady Goring with mock asperity. "That *malevolent* animal will be out of my house. Perhaps I may keep my cook after all."

While Susan puzzled over the meaning of "malevolent" and prepared to defend her pet, Nick said, "We should leave him here. He will kill all the birds within two miles."

"Nick!" Susan glared at him. "Daisy will do no such thing. She loves birds!"

"To eat," her brother mumbled into his plate, but he did not take up the argument.

"Rex will keep the cat away from the coveys," said William.

"Mama! You will not let William's dog hurt Daisy, will you?" appealed Susan.

"It would probably be the other way about," murmured Nick.

"No one will hurt your cat, Susan," replied Anabel. "But you must try to train, er, her better. Daisy is a little wild."

"*I* think she's perfect," declared the youngest Wyndham.

Her brothers glared at her as if to say this was only natural, considering her own temperament. All the adults laughed.

"Do you see what you are taking on?" dared Lady Goring.

Christopher met her eyes, his own twinkling. "With great joy." He and Anabel exchanged a fond look. Georgina's smile trembled a little.

"What do you mean?" asked Nicholas, his eyes moving intelligently from one to the other.

"Nothing, dear." Anabel suppressed her smile. It was not the time to make their announcement. "Here is a Chantilly cream, your favorite."

Nick was diverted but not fooled. During the rest of the meal he often glanced from his mother to Christopher and back again.

When they finished, the party gathered in the drawing room for a very successful, and noisy, game of lottery tickets. Georgina soon forgot her sadness in the excitement of it, and she looked much younger than her eighteen years as she dickered with the children for counters. Even Lady Goring, who had joined in only after much persuasion, enjoyed herself hugely. And Susan, who came out the winner, could hardly be torn from the table to go to bed. Indeed, she resisted mightily, and would have gone on playing all night if allowed.

At last, however, the children followed Nurse upstairs, leaving the older members of the party in the drawing room. Lady Goring sighed and stretched her arms. "What a pleasant evening. Who would have thought we should enjoy a silly game so much?"

Georgina agreed. "I have not played lottery tickets for five years."

"I feel quite exhausted by it. I believe I shall go straight up to bed. Are you coming, Georgina?" The girl rose and joined her aunt. "Good night, Christopher," added Lady Goring. "We will see you again tomorrow?"

"Yes."

"Splendid." Amid a chorus of farewells, they went out.

"Are you very tired?" Hanford asked Anabel, going to sit close to her on the sofa.

"A little."

"You should sleep." He touched her cheek gently with his fingertips.

"Soon." She looked into his blue eyes. "I am very happy, Christopher."

"As am I."

"I feel so fortunate, being prevented from making such a mistake."

"Not half so fortunate as I!"

They laughed.

"We should make plans. When will you go home?"

"Soon. But there is no need to decide anything tonight. Tomorrow will be better, when you are rested."

Anabel nodded and rested her head comfortably on his shoulder. "But I am eager to leave now."

He kissed the top of her head. They remained so for a while, Hanford feeling a great contentment spread through him. He could not remember being so happy. "I think Nick suspects us," he said finally. Anabel did not reply and, looking down, he saw that she was fast asleep. He smiled, then eased his arm from behind her and went to ring for the maid to take her upstairs.

Chapter Sixteen

Anabel woke the following morning with a sense of oppression, and she lay in bed for a while wondering why. Everything was wonderful. She and Christopher and the children were going to be tremendously happy. She glowed at the mere thought of it. Then she remembered Sir Charles. Today she must face him and break off their engagement; that was what weighed on her. He would be very angry, she knew, and she had always shrunk from acrimonious scenes, preferring to agree rather than to argue. She had seen how he resented any interference with his wishes, and although she didn't have any great faith in his love for her, she knew that he was determined on the marriage. Perhaps, she thought, he did love her in a way. But his sort of love was wholly selfish, a matter of his own desires and visions alone. Somehow she conformed to his image of a wife, and he was set on placing her in that position. He would not give up his plan without a battle. How different from Christopher!

For a while she drifted in a pleasant reverie, recounting Christopher's sterling qualities. She was brought abruptly back to earth by the entrance of her maid with tea, the drawing of the curtains, and the other familiar rituals of rising. What would she say to Norbury? she wondered as her hair was brushed. How would it be best to begin?

This question threw her into the dismals again. Anabel was still far from accustomed to upholding her own decisions. The knowledge that she loved Christopher and had made a mistake with Norbury had been almost instinctive. It was quite another matter to plan rationally how best to convey that news and bear down opposition. She did not question her choice—far from it but she was uneasy about her ability to explain it. Her first marriage had been so much simpler. Her father had presented a fait accompli, and she had merely acquiesced. There had been no necessity for explanations. And Norbury had been much the same. He had impressed his will on her and expected her to yield, as she had. This time all was different. *She* had decided, and it was up to her to take the actions that would bring her own happiness.

Briefly Anabel wished for Christopher. If only he could be with her today, to confront Sir Charles at her side. But that was impossible, she knew. It would make everything ten times worse. In any case, this was her tangle. She had been foolish, and she must right her mistake. Anabel sensed that it was very important for her to see this matter through alone. This season in London had been good for her, she realized. It had shown her a great many things about herself, and she must use this new knowledge rather than retreat into outworn habits. She and Christopher would help each other. She would not rely on him for every decision.

This train of thought was fascinating, if not very comforting, and Anabel remained distracted throughout breakfast, not even hearing the remarks Lady Goring and Georgina addressed to her. After a while they exchanged a glance and abandoned the attempt at conversation, talking quietly to each other. Anabel ate little and soon went up to the drawing room to wait and think. She still had not determined how she would speak to Norbury. Should she simply plunge in as soon as he arrived, or should she wait for an opening? He would bring up their wedding date again; perhaps she could begin there.

Pacing back and forth across the drawing-room carpet, Anabel twisted her hands nervously. It was all very well to vow to change. In actuality it was very difficult.

The sound of the bell made her jump. She heard a footman going to the door and voices below. It was Sir Charles. Her heart speeded up, and she took a deep breath, going to the sofa and sitting down, trying to appear calm and collected.

"Good morning," said Norbury from the drawing-room doorway. "Are you more rested today? It is so pleasant, I thought we might go for a drive." He came toward her, smiling, and took her hand. "It will do you good to get out."

"Oh . . . I . . ." Anabel felt confused. All her faculties had been concentrated on the coming confrontation. She didn't want to go out; she wanted to get it over as soon as possible. But she couldn't seem to think of objections.

"Come," said Norbury. "It is really a lovely morning. You will enjoy being out." He continued to smile pleasantly. He knew that he had not come off well in the events of the last few days. He had allowed his temper to get the best of him again, and Anabel had been annoyed. He was anxious to erase this damaging memory and remind her of his manifold attractions. It would be a simple matter, he felt, to drive the uninteresting Mr. Hanford out of her mind.

"I would prefer to stay here," managed Anabel.

"Nonsense. This is only because you have not been out and seen the day. I insist. Go and fetch your hat."

"But—"

Slightly annoyed but feigning laughter, he took her shoulders and marched her toward the door. "I won't hear it. You will thank me in the end, wait and see."

Defeated, Anabel went upstairs and got out a bonnet and shawl. She could not summon the energy to fight Norbury on this; she was saving it for the larger issue.

It was indeed a lovely day, the air soft and fragrant and the sky a brilliant blue. Norbury had his phaeton, and as he helped Anabel into it he told the groom holding the horses that he might wait here for their return. This, at least, was a relief, Anabel thought. It would have been impossible to talk with a servant hanging on behind.

They started off briskly through the busy streets. "A turn around the park?" asked Sir Charles, and she nodded, her thoughts still on what lay ahead. They said little during the short journey to the gates. Norbury was occupied with driving, and Anabel was abstracted. But when they turned into the quieter avenues of the park, he said, "I hope the children are completely recovered from their adventures?"

"What? Oh, yes, they are well."

"I realized that I never actually heard where they had got to." He was determined to counteract her previous impressions.

"Uh, the boys went after Susan." Anabel couldn't concentrate on this when she was continually wondering how to bring up their engagement.

"Went after?"

Seeing that he was not going to leave the subject, she quickly explained what had happened. Her references to Christopher were inevitably warm.

Norbury carefully ignored them. "I see. Well, I am very glad it is all straightened out again. I know you were terribly worried."

She nodded.

"It is time I saw the children again," he added. "Perhaps we might take them out tomorrow?" He put all the eagerness he could muster in his voice. Though this was the last thing he wanted to do, he felt it was necessary to restore his position.

"No."

He glanced at her, surprised.

"They are being punished for going out without leave," she continued cravenly, intimidated by his look. "They are not to have outings."

"Ah." He was relieved. "I suppose that is wise."

Anabel was berating herself for avoiding the true reason behind her refusal. She had to get it over with. "I must speak to you about something," she blurted out.

"Yes?"

"It . . . it is very difficult. I don't know precisely how to begin, so I shall simply say it. I wish to end our engagement, Charles."

"What?" He spoke blankly, as if he had not understood her words.

"I am very sorry, but I do not think we shall suit after all. It is my fault. I made a mistake. And I sincerely apologize for any pain I may have—"

"Are you joking?" He still seemed chiefly astonished.

"N-no. I—"

"I suppose Hanford is behind this. He put you up to it, and because you are grateful for his rescue of your children, you agreed. You do not really mean it."

"That is not true!" Anabel was flustered. This was not how she had expected things to go. She had not thought Christopher would come into it, and she could not precisely deny that he was behind it, though not as Sir Charles claimed.

"Have you thought that he may have arranged the whole crisis merely to win your sympathy?" asked Norbury.

"What?"

"You say your daughter went to him. How do you know that? Perhaps he took her from the house, knowing that your sons would follow. Or perhaps he simply took the three of them, taught them what to say, and brought them back at the proper moment to earn your gratitude." He warmed to this idea. "Yes. He would wait just long enough so that you would fall into his arms when he returned them."

"That's ridiculous!"

"You didn't fall into his arms?" inquired Sir Charles sarcastically and, seeing Anabel's expression, added, "Naturally you did. I'm sure he counted on that."

"He did no such thing!"

"Indeed? You are not breaking off our engagement to marry Hanford, then?"

She hesitated. Would it be better to tell him or not?

But he saw the answer in her face, and was at once filled with a murderous rage. "I see. His little plot has succeeded. Or so he believes."

"There was no plot. Christopher would never do what you suggest. He is not that sort of person."

"Is he not?" Norbury sneered.

"No! I have known him for years."

"Yet only now have you decided to marry him. Odd."

For a brief moment Anabel was shaken by doubt. Was it possible that he was right? Christopher had said that he was desperate over her engagement. Could he have planned to end it this way? But the thought was no sooner considered than rejected. He would do no such thing; she knew it. "It is of no consequence what you think. You are wrong. And this has nothing to do with my decision. I am breaking it off."

"This is not the time to discuss it. Wait a few days, until your anxiety over your children has faded. You will see then that you are being hasty." It was his last attempt at appeal.

"No, I will not. I am quite certain."

Sir Charles' rage flooded him. How dared she speak to him so? he thought. He had done her the unique honor of offering his hand, and now she was throwing it aside as if it meant nothing—and for a nonentity like Hanford! *His* plans and wishes were to be swept aside so that these two could have their way. He was to be balked of the woman he had chosen and the life he had envisioned. It was intolerable! Did she not realize that he might have had any woman in London? Yet he had chosen her, despite her widowhood and her pack of whining brats. He *would* have what he wanted. "I refuse," he said.

"What?" Anabel didn't know what he meant.

"I refuse to allow you to dissolve the engagement. I won't agree to it."

"What do you mean? You must."

"Why?"

"Well . . . that is . . ."

"If *I* were the one who wished to break my promise, society would protest," he countered. "It would not be 'the act of a gentleman' to draw back. Yet you may do as you please in the matter. Well, I will not go along. We *shall* be married."

"You would marry me even though I do not wish it?" Anabel was astounded and confused. She had never imagined such a response to her announcement.

"You will come round eventually." His tone was smug, and he spoke as if the matter were settled.

"You're mad. I certainly will not. And you cannot force me to marry you. I shall send a notice to the *Morning Post* today saying that our engagement is at an end. And now I want to go home. Turn around!"

She expected another angry outburst, but Norbury merely frowned thoughtfully. Thinking he was reconsidering his ridiculous ultimatum, she added, "We should be very unhappy, Charles. You would regret it as much as I. When you have thought over the matter, you will see that."

He said nothing. He was gazing out over the horses' heads as if weighing some idea.

"We are not at all suited," continued Anabel hopefully. "I find I do not care to live in town, and you are not overfond of children, I think. Your mother was not pleased with the match."

"Nonsense!" he snapped.

Anabel abandoned this line. "You deserve someone who can take a place in society to match your own. I could not." He was ignoring her again. Anabel gazed at his set profile and wished fervently that she had not come out with him. At home she could ask him to leave; here she was trapped. "Truly, Charles, you will be glad in a very few days."

With a sudden jerk on the reins, he turned the phaeton left, then left again into another avenue, heading back the way they had come. Anabel breathed a sigh of relief and relaxed a little in her seat.

They drove in silence for a while. Anabel was happy to have things over and wary of upsetting the balance established, and Norbury was too angry to speak. He had never in his life been put aside by a woman he deigned to distinguish, and to have this occur when he had actually proposed marriage was more than he could bear.

Outside the park, he turned into a busy street and wove in and out among wagons, carts, and pedestrians. Anabel sat slumped beside him, ignoring the spectacle, waiting to be home again. She was thinking how fortunate it was that she and Christopher did not want to live in London. She could not have faced Norbury day after day and maintained a pretense of polite indifference. When would they reach her mother's? she wondered. Looking around, she was startled. "Where are you going?"

Norbury did not reply.

"This is not the way back. We should have turned long since. What are you doing?"

He ignored her, guiding the phaeton past a wide lumber cart.

"Charles!" Anabel gazed about, trying to identify the street.

"This is another way home," said Norbury.

"I don't believe you! Turn around at once."

In answer, he urged the horses forward at a faster pace.

"If you don't turn around, I shall jump off."

He laughed a little. "No, you won't. You would be seriously injured on the cobbles, if not killed."

Anabel looked at the pavement rushing by beneath them and tried to steel herself to leap. She couldn't. He was trying to frighten her as a punishment, she decided. If she refused to be intimidated, he would give it up and take her home. She sat back with folded arms and stared stonily ahead.

But Norbury merely drove on, satisfied with her silence. They left the neighborhood of the park and the fashionable part of London, and continued into an area of small houses, neat but by no means elegant. Anabel had never been here before. Her resolve wavered. "Charles, where are we going?"

He didn't answer.

"Why are you doing this? I shan't change my mind. Can you not be a little charitable and . . ."

With a quick jerk on the reins, he pulled up. The horses plunged and reared. And before Anabel could gather her wits to jump down, his hand had closed firmly on her upper arm, keeping her in her seat. "Here, you," he said to a grubby boy standing on the pavement below. "Go to their heads." He was holding the startled team with one hand. The boy ran and took the bridles.

"Let go of me!" demanded Anabel.

In response, he pushed her before him out of the phaeton, almost knocking her to the ground from its high perch. She struggled, but his grip on her arm was cruelly tight; she could not break it.

"Hold them for me," he told the boy, then pushed her toward the narrow brick house in front of them.

Anabel struggled harder. He transferred his grip from her arm to her waist, pinning her against him and propelling her up two steps to the front door. She hit at him as he took a ring of keys from his pocket and applied one to the lock, but he paid no heed. "Help!" she cried, twisting her head to try to see the boy. There was no one else visible in the street. "Help me! Get someone."

The child merely gaped at her. Sir Charles flung open the door and pushed her into a narrow hall, slamming the panel behind him.

"Have you gone mad?" asked Anabel. "What do you think you are doing?"

In one quick movement he gathered her wrists in one hand behind her back. Then he forced her forward again, up two sets of twisting stairs. Anabel exerted all her strength to break away. She strained against his grip, threw herself from one side to the other in hope of overbalancing him, and kicked at him with her feet, all to no avail. He was amazingly strong. Nothing she could do seemed to have any effect on him.

He paused on the second landing to open a door there. Then he forced her into a small bedchamber and released her. Anabel backed away from him, chafing her bruised wrists. He remained between her and the door.

"This is a house I sometimes use," he said. "You will stay here."

"What are you doing?" she cried. "You are mad!"

"On the contrary, I am carrying out an extremely rational plan to make you keep your promise. You will remain here until tomorrow, at which time I will escort you home. Having been away all night in my company, as it will appear, you will have to marry me." He looked complacent.

Anabel's blue eyes widened. "What? You . . . you . . ."

"No harm will come to you. This house is perfectly safe; it is a very respectable neighborhood." He smiled a little.

"I will never marry you!"

"Oh, I think you will. Your friend Hanford may not be quite so attentive when he knows you have spent the night with me. And the scandal would be shocking. Your children would suffer if you refused me."

Anabel flushed with rage. How dare he mention her children? "I will take them back to the country. We shall do very well there."

Norbury shrugged. "We will discuss it further in the morning. I think you will change your mind. And now there are some arrangements I must make, if you will excuse me."

"How can you wish to marry in this way?" cried Anabel. "Do you want a wife who hates you? Because that is what I should be, if we ever married."

He met her eyes. "Oh, I think you would put that aside quite soon. You are overwrought now, and you have been worried in the last few days. When you are calmer, you will see things differently. You *did* accept me, after all. You did not hate me then, and you do not now. You have simply allowed your concern for your children to cloud your mind, and Hanford took advantage of that."

"Nonsense! I had grave doubts even before the children ran away, and I am certain I would have broken it off in any case."

He frowned and took a step toward her. "You do not mean that. You are angry with me and trying to wound."

"I do mean it!"

But he shook his head. "When you have had time to think, you will change your mind. I have no wish to hurt you, Anabel. Nothing will happen to you here. And I take such extreme measures only because I love you and cannot bear to lose you."

"Love," she repeated derisively. "You do not know the meaning of the word!"

His fists clenched, then relaxed. "You are mistaken. I do love you. I have never wished to marry a woman in my life before."

"What you call love is just another form of selfishness. If you love me, you would put my happiness before yours and let me go." She saw his eyes flicker and felt a sudden hope.

Then he said, "You will be happy with me." And before she could speak again, he turned and strode out of the room, locking the door behind him.

Chapter Seventeen

Anabel was furious. She couldn't remember ever having been so angry in her life. She had been suppressing her own reactions in the hope that reason would sway Norbury, but now they surged up. She ran to the door and listened to his footsteps retreat down the stairs. "I shall never marry you!" she cried, pounding her fist on the panels.

There was no response. She tried the lock and found it firm, then ran to the single window at the opposite end of the room and looked out. The distance to the street was intimidating, and when she pushed on the sash to open it and get a better view, she found it was immovable. She could break the glass, she thought, sitting back on her heels, but she could not see how that would do her any good. There was a floor above this, so she was not near the roof. And she doubted that she could climb to safety from the shattered window.

Standing, she went to the only article of furniture in the chamber—a bare, narrow bed—and sat down. Charles might do as he liked, she told herself; he would accomplish nothing. She might be forced to remain here until tomorrow, but she would do nothing else. She would *not* marry him. She would go home as she had planned, with Christopher and the children. He would believe her and stand by her, she was certain. And if scandal arose, they would simply ignore it. They could be happy without society if need be.

Resolutely pushing aside doubts about her children's future under these circumstances, she rose again and paced the narrow confines of the chamber. If only there were some way she could get word home. Or if she had not consented to go out with Charles in the first place. But though she had had a low opinion of him, she had never suspected he would try something so despicable. She still could not quite believe that he would wish to marry a woman who despised him.

Remembering something, she went to the window again and gazed out. The boy who had held Norbury's horses was gone, as was his carriage. If she could attract the attention of some passerby, perhaps he would take a message for her. She bent and slipped off her shoe, grasped the toe firmly, and rapped the glass with the heel. Nothing happened. She hit it again, harder. The pane cracked. Abandoning caution, she struck once more with all her strength, shattering first one square, then two more. When she stopped, she had three small openings surrounded by jagged spears of glass, and she eyed them doubtingly. She couldn't get her head out. It would be very difficult to stop anyone by shouting from this height. Nonetheless, she must try. Putting on her shoe, she suddenly recalled that she had no way of writing a message or any money to offer the carrier. She had come out with little more than a handkerchief. Discouraged, she sat on the bed again and tried to think what to do.

Sir Charles, meantime, was removing his carriage to a livery nearby, where he could leave it out of sight. His plans were not yet fully formed—he had acted on impulse—

so he was also thinking furiously. He could not go home; indeed, he could not go to any of his usual haunts in London. He must not be seen until tomorrow. But he could communicate with his servants. As he thought of this, a self-satisfied smile dawned on his dark features. Yes, that was it. At the livery, he asked for pen and paper, and was dubiously led to a small office and supplied with very inferior examples. Still smiling, he composed a note to his valet—the only personal servant he kept—informing him that he and Lady Wyndham had decided to elope, and that he was to tell no one of their plan. As he sealed this missive and offered one of the stableboys a coin to deliver it, his smile widened. Turvey was constitutionally incapable of keeping anything to himself, and this irritating trait would be very convenient today. The news would undoubtedly leak out; Anabel would be trapped.

When he had finished, it was well past midday. Norbury adjourned to a tavern in the neighborhood, where he was most unlikely to meet anyone he knew. To make certain, he took a private parlor and settled contentedly to cold meat and claret. He would pass the day here, he decided, perhaps even take a room. It would be easier to carry out his plan if he did not have to face Anabel. Her final accusations had shaken him more than he would admit. Pushing this thought aside, he called for another bottle.

Christopher Hanford called at Lady Goring's at three, to hear from Anabel how her talk with Norbury had gone, and was very surprised to be told that none of the ladies were at home. Frowning at the footman who had given him this news, he said, "Are you certain of that? My name is Hanford, and I believe Lady Wyndham is expecting me."

"I'm sorry, sir. She isn't here." The servant's normally impassive face showed a tremor of some emotion, but he merely waited, holding the door.

"Uncle Christopher!" hissed a voice from farther along the hall, and Nick's head appeared from the library. "Come here."

The footman looked uncertain. Hanford brushed past him and strode into the room. "Nick? What are you doing down here? Where is your mother?"

The boy pulled him forward and shut the door. His face looked pinched, and his blue eyes were worried. "*She's* run away," he whispered.

"What?"

"Quiet! I'm not supposed to know, and I don't want William or Susan to hear. They may be looking for me."

"What are you talking about?" asked Hanford in a lower voice.

"I heard Grandmama telling Georgina before luncheon. Mama went out with Sir Charles Norbury, and she didn't come back. They have gone out to look for her." Nicholas was puzzled and dejected. "Do you think she ran away with him? She told us she wasn't going to marry him after all, but perhaps she changed her mind, and she didn't want to tell us because she knew we would be unhappy. We should never have objected to—"

"Nonsense!" snapped Hanford, his fists clenching and unclenching at his sides. "It is nothing like that."

"You think not?" The boy was hopeful.

Hanford became aware of the resolutely suppressed fear in his eyes. "I'm certain it is just a mistake," he replied firmly. "Your mother forgot to tell them of another engagement, I daresay. She will be home for dinner."

"That's what Grandmama said," replied Nick doubtfully, "but she didn't sound sure."

"What else did she say?"

"Well, they said Mama had gone out driving with Sir Charles at eleven, and that she should have been back hours ago." He glanced at the clock on the mantelpiece. "It's three now."

"They went *driving*?" Nick stared, and Hanford controlled himself. "Anything else?"

"No. But Grandmama seemed worried."

"Everything will be all right. But you mustn't speak to anyone else about this."

Nicholas shook his head, frowning.

"I will be back later today."

"Are you going after her?" He sounded hopeful again.

"It is not a question of that. I have some business." Hanford stalked out, and Nick watched him with unallayed worry in his face.

As soon as he was out of the house Christopher gave way to rage. It was obvious to him what had happened. Anabel had tried to break it off, and Norbury had made away with her. *Why* had she gone out with him? She might have known . . . but he paused, just even in his fury. She could not have predicted that the man would act this way. Even he had not imagined such villainy.

Seeing a hackney cab, he signaled it to stop. He would have to find them and bring her back. But before he did, he would teach Sir Charles Norbury the lesson of his life. The idea made him smile humorlessly.

He overcame the first obstacle—his ignorance of Norbury's address—with ease, obtaining it from an acquaintance at White's. But when he pulled up before Norbury's lodgings in Ryder Street and knocked, he was told by the retired gentleman's gentleman who looked after the chambers that Sir Charles was out. "This is a matter of great urgency," replied Hanford. "Is anyone in his rooms? I must find him."

198

Something in his eyes seemed to impress the man. "His valet Turvey is here. Would you wish to speak with him?"

"Yes!"

The other drew back. "This way."

Turvey, who was pressing a coat in the kitchen, was startled at the interruption, for Hanford had insisted upon accompanying the man downstairs. When asked for his master's whereabouts, he gaped and bridled. "I'm sure I don't know," he answered. But he exchanged a speaking look with the proprietor.

Christopher was in no mood for evasions. Stepping forward, he grasped the valet's neckcloth and pulled it tight, shaking him slightly. "Tell me where he is!" he said between his teeth.

Turvey choked and gabbled. "Sir!" exclaimed the other man. "Please, sir!"

Hanford merely shook Turvey again, watching the man's face purple with savage satisfaction.

Turvey goggled desperately at his friend, who held out his hands in helpless query, then croaked, "He's eloped."

"What?" Hanford let go, and the man fell in a heap.

"With Lady Wyndham, to whom he is engaged," added the valet haughtily, readjusting his collar. Now that the news was out, he seemed to savor his superior knowledge. "Very romantic, ain't it?" He smirked.

Christopher bent over him. "If you dare to repeat that tale to anyone, I shall make you regret it. Do you understand me?" He took his lapels again and shook him.

Turvey gaped again, turning pale at what he saw in Hanford's eyes.

"Where is the groom who went out with Sir Charles this morning?"

Turvey's mouth dropped open. Hanford looked murderous.

"Round in the stables," said the other man, who had been increasingly worried. He was eager to get Hanford out of his house before he caused some damage.

Christopher released the valet. "And where might that be?"

"In the mews." He pointed toward the rear of the house.

"Does that door go through to them?"

Reluctantly the proprietor nodded, and Hanford pushed past them and out. Turvey, rubbing his neck, met the other's eyes. "A rum go, and no mistake," he said.

His companion agreed. "I wonder if your master's finally met his match, Turvey. That gentleman was in a fine rage, he was."

The valet nodded, and the two of them contemplated the probable outcome with avid eyes.

In the stables, after one look at the groom, Hanford gave up violence for monetary persuasion, and he was soon informed of the circumstances of the morning drive and of the fact that the phaeton had not returned. Picturing a high-perch phaeton on the country roads, Christopher shook his head. "Your master has another place in London, does he not?" he asked. "A house somewhere he uses? You have driven him there."

"Have I, guv?"

Hanford held out a ten-pound note, and the man raised his eyebrows. "Happen I have."

"What is the address?"

The groom looked at him, then at the money. He grinned and told him.

Hanford left Ryder Street almost weak with relief. He had hazarded everything on a theory, and it had paid off. Anabel was in that house; he knew it. It had been the only possible explanation. Norbury could not drive an unwilling woman out of town in a phaeton, and he could not have taken her to a public inn. Now it remained only to get there and free her. In another hackney, Christopher cursed every cart and pedestrian that delayed his progress to her.

Chapter Eighteen

Norbury poured the last of the second bottle of claret in the late afternoon. He sat at his ease in the inn parlor, his legs stretched out, turning the wineglass by the stem and watching the light dance in the ruby liquid. He was not foxed, but the fumes of the wine surrounded his brain and filled it with self-congratulatory images. He remembered past triumphs and pleasures; he recalled the series of mistresses he had kept in the small house where his future wife now waited. The juxtaposition amused him. It seemed somehow apt. He had dismissed the last occupant soon after he had offered for Anabel, feeling extremely virtuous and domestic, but the lease had several months to run, and he had done nothing about getting rid of it. Now it was serving a final purpose.

He wondered what Anabel was doing and, in thinking about her, frowned. He was a bit disappointed in his promised bride; she had limitations he had not seen until today. How could any woman prefer Hanford to him? The man was a nobody, a country squire without pretensions to fashion or *ton*. He had no wit and, as far as

Norbury had seen, little intelligence. He was like a thousand others. Norbury could only conclude, as he had told Anabel, that Hanford had tricked her. He had played upon her maternal feelings in a vulnerable moment. The more Norbury thought about it, the more certain he was that Hanford had staged the children's disappearance, then used it to his own advantage. It was the only possible explanation.

Still, Anabel should not have been so easily taken in. She was absurdly attached to those children. It came of shutting herself up with them in the country for so many years. Her perceptions had become distorted. But that would soon change. Norbury sipped his wine, smiling slightly. He had no doubt whatever of his ability to bring Anabel around to his own way of thinking. He had done as much so many times in the past. Women had resisted him or rebelled against his strictures, but in the end, they had capitulated to his powerful personality and physical charms. In the one or two cases where they had not, he had abandoned the field in disdain.

Anabel would soon change her tone, when he was able to exert the full force of his persuasive powers. He had been hampered with her, as he had not with his mistresses, by convention and propriety. Once they were wed, she would be very pleased that he had not let her break it off.

His smile widening, Norbury imagined the scene. There was always a thrill in overcoming a woman's initial opposition, and in this case it would have a particular spice, for his feelings for Anabel were truly quite strong. In a way he loved her, and drawing out her eager response would be vastly exciting. The picture, heightened by the claret, inflamed him, and he suddenly realized that there was no need to wait. Anabel was his now. Transfixed, he gazed at the wall of the tavern parlor. His determination to marry her remained firm—they *would* marry, and soon—thus they were practically married already. And how much easier it would be to have a willing, fervent bride than to force her through the ceremony. He would make her see her mistake first, now.

His pale green eyes gleaming, Norbury stood and tossed off the last of the wine. Leaving a few coins on the table, he retrieved his hat and strode out into the street. The afternoon was waning; dusk was near. It would be the perfect time for a seduction. His expression eager, he set off to walk the short distance to the house.

Anabel watched the day ending with resignation. She had run the gamut of emotions as it passed, from anger to hope to despair. She had had no luck in attracting the attention of passersby. Those who had heard her calling through the broken window had ignored her, and most had shown no sign of even hearing. Now she was simply waiting for this outrage to end. She knew what she would do tomorrow—depart for home at once—and she had finally admitted that there was nothing to be done before that.

She was lying on the narrow bed, hoping for sleep to make the time pass more quickly, when she heard the footsteps on the stairs. She sat up at once and listened; she had not expected Norbury to return before morning. Could this be someone else? She stood and moved around the bed, putting it between her and the door.

The lock clicked, and he came in, scanning the dim room for her and smiling when he saw her position. "Anabel, my dear. Are you comfortable?" With a twist of his hand, he relocked the door, putting the key in an inner pocket.

"Why have you come back?" She didn't like his tone.

"To see that you are all right, of course. I was worried you might be frightened, all alone in an empty house."

"I should be much better at home. Perhaps you've reconsidered this ridiculous scheme?"

He shook his head, still smiling, and moved closer.

"It is not going to work, you know. I shall weather the scandal. I prefer it to marrying you." He didn't seem to hear. He stepped still nearer, and Anabel caught the scent of wine. For the first time a hint of fear shot through her. In the gathering twilight Norbury seemed very large and strong. What did he mean to do? "I thought you were coming back in the morning," she added.

"A better plan occurred to me."

He was very close now, and Anabel straightened, refusing to cower in the corner. "What better plan?"

Instead of answering, he moved swiftly, catching her shoulders and pulling her against him, his lips fastening irresistibly on hers. He propelled her backward toward the wall and imprisoned her body with his.

Anabel twisted and struggled, but she could not break free. When she brought her hands up to claw at him, he grasped her wrists and encircled them with one of his behind her back. She could not even avoid his kiss; he kept his lips on hers and pressed her head against the wall. His free hand roved about her body, teasing and seeking to inflame, expert in the ways of passion. She could feel his excitement growing, and she stopped struggling, fearing that her resistance increased rather than quenched his desire.

Norbury felt it and laughed a little. "You see? You were wrong. I am the man for you." His voice was thick with desire, and he began to force her around the headboard to the bed.

Anabel, frantic, suddenly remembered the key. It was in his pocket; she had seen him put it there. If she could get it away . . . Slowly, so as not to arouse his suspicions, she relaxed in his arms. Norbury laughed again and released her wrists, the other hand fondling her breast as he buried his face in her neck. Anabel carefully moved her hands along his sides and across the lapels of his coat. It was the left waistcoat pocket, she was sure.

In another moment she had the key! She threw all her strength into one effort to break his hold, and failed. It didn't even loosen. Indeed, her momentary lapse had allowed him to maneuver her to the bed, and now he forced her down upon it, covering her body with his. "The key, eh?" he murmured. "Keep it, and see if you want to use it after a while." One of his hands pulled at her skirts and moved up her leg under them; the other remained on her breast.

Anabel saw that her tactics had been to no avail, and she struggled desperately again. It was no use; he was too strong. "I hate you!" she cried. "And I always shall, whatever happens."

He raised his head, surprised. He had thought she would be yielding by now. He kissed her throat, her lips, her forehead; she remained rigid, her face turned away. Reining in his passion, he redoubled his efforts to arouse her, using every trick he had gleaned in a long and varied amorous career. She was unmoved. Puzzled, Norbury drew a little away, while keeping a firm hold on her, and looked into her eyes. She looked back at him with fear and contempt.

They stared at each other for a moment, neither in the least understanding what was in the other's mind. Then the tension was broken by a rhythmic crashing sound downstairs. The volume increased to a crescendo; there was a splintering of wood, then the sound of running footsteps on the stairs.

Norbury sat up with a jerk. He twisted the key from Anabel's hand and rose, listening to the noise with a scowl.

"Anabel!" called a male voice. "Anabel!"

"Christopher!" she cried, sitting up also. "Here I am."

The footsteps pounded to a stop outside the door of the room. "Are you all right? Can you open the door?"

"No, it's locked and—"

"I have the key," roared Norbury, striding toward the entry. His brief puzzlement had exploded into rage at this appearance of his rival and the thwarting of his desire. Whatever qualms he had felt had been swept away. He felt murderous.

The door shook under a heavy blow, then, at a second blow, the hinges on the ancient, poorly made door ripped from their foundation and Christopher burst through. "To the rescue once again, eh?" sneered Sir Charles.

With an inarticulate cry of rage, Hanford threw himself upon the man, and they fell together and rolled over and over on the dusty floor. Anabel stood and looked for a weapon, but there was none. She strained forward, trying to decipher the tangle of limbs in the fading light. Each man had his hands locked around the other's throat, and Norbury was gouging Christopher with his knees. She stepped forward, hoping to help him, but they rolled again at that moment, and she could get no clear opening.

The battle was all but silent. The only sound in the room was the ragged breathing of the combatants, very loud in that enclosed space. Suddenly Norbury twisted and straddled Christopher, his grip on his throat tightening. Christoper heaved ineffectually.

Anabel, seeing her chance, darted forward and struck Norbury's head with all the strength in her arm. The blow did not really hurt him, but it surprised him so that he slackened his grip on Hanford, who immediately reversed their positions, pinning Norbury to the ground. The latter gazed at Anabel, stunned by her action.

Christopher's blue eyes burned with rage. His hands tightened until Norbury made strangled choking noises and clawed at his fingers desperately. "Christopher!" cried Anabel. "Don't *kill* him!"

Her voice brought him upright, and he drew his hands back and gazed at them as if seeing them for the first time. Norbury did not take advantage of the opening. He lay where he was, rubbing his neck and scowling.

"Let us go home, Christopher," urged Anabel, putting a hand on his arm.

Dazed, he nodded and rose, stepping away from Sir Charles' prone figure.

"You hit me," said the latter, slowly sitting up and gazing at Anabel.

She turned away from him.

"You *really* prefer him to me." It was not a question, but he sounded astonished.

"Yes, I do!" she snapped, pulling again at Christopher's arm. "Please, let's go."

Hanford rubbed his face with his hands. It was difficult to move from a murderous rage to normality; he felt disoriented. And the fact that he had been perfectly ready to kill Sir Charles still stunned him. With a massive effort he recovered himself. "Yes. By all means, let us go." He turned to Norbury, who remained on the floor. "A notice of the dissolution of your engagement will appear in tomorrow's *Morning Post*. If you try to create a scandal, I—"

"I shan't." He shook his head with weary incredulity. "I can see when I am beaten."

Anabel and Christopher left him sitting there and hurried from the room.

Chapter Nineteen

At the bottom of the stairs, seeing that Norbury did not intend to follow them, Christopher and Anabel fell into each other's arms. A great wave of relief and happiness washed over Anabel as she rested there, and she nearly cried at the joy of their reunion. How could she ever have overlooked Christopher's perfections? she wondered again. He was everything she wanted in a man.

"Are you all right?" he said.

"Yes, I am perfectly all right now."

"I came as soon as I could. It took a deucedly long time to find out about this house."

She raised her head from his shoulder. "How did you find it?"

"I knew you must be in London, so I bribed his groom to tell me where." He shrugged, and she smiled. "Come, I must get you home. They are worried." Keeping an arm around her, he started toward the door, then stopped.

"What is it?"

"We have no carriage. I took a hack." He looked so chagrined that Anabel burst out laughing. After a moment's indignation Christopher started to smile, then he laughed with her. The tensions both had experienced during this day were released in great gusts of merriment, and at last they had to hang on each other to keep from doubling over with laughter.

"Sir Charles will think we have gone mad," gasped Anabel.

"Fortunately we do not care a whit what he thinks," responded Hanford, trying to catch his breath.

Their eyes met, and they both laughed again, more moderately, each thinking that there was no one else in the world with whom he could have shared this amusement.

"Not a proper rescue at all," added Christopher. "The knight in shining armor always has his horse. But I have been rushing about London without a plan, so frantic to find you that my brain was addled." His smile died. "Indeed, I have never felt such terror. If I had not discovered where you were . . ." He shook his head.

Anabel nodded, also sobering. She did not want to think of what would have happened if he had not come when he did.

"I was truly ready to murder him," continued Hanford thoughtfully. "It is a daunting prospect."

Their eyes met again, serious. Without words, they communicated their love for each other.

"Let us find another hack," said Anabel, taking his arm. "It will be an adventure. I have never ridden in one before."

Arm in arm, they left the house and walked along the darkening street until Christopher saw a hackney cab and signaled it to stop. They sat close together on the drive home, holding hands but saying little, and when they climbed down before Lady Goring's town house, Anabel paused to look at it. "I feel as if I've been away for days," she said.

He nodded. "It seems a long time since I came to call on you here; yet it is only a few hours." He rang the bell, and they were admitted by an eager footman, who looked as if he would very much like to ask what had happened.

"Is my mother at home?" asked Anabel.

"Yes, my lady. She is—" He was interrupted by the sudden appearance of Susan on the landing above. She surveyed the hall, and the newcomers, and started determinedly down.

"Have you seen William down here?" she asked.

"No," said Anabel. "What are you—"

"Or Georgina?"

"We have just come in." The prosaic welcome made Anabel smile a little.

"I know *someone* came down," replied her daughter. "I heard them. Do you think it was Grandmama?" Seeing their uncomprehending looks, she added, "We are playing hide and seek."

"Grandmama, too?" asked Anabel, amazed.

Susan shrugged. "It was Nick's idea. He insisted that everyone play."

Christopher and Anabel exchanged a glance. He had told her of Nicholas' knowledge of her disappearance.

A sudden scrabbling sound made them all look up. Daisy was galloping down the stairs, his ginger fur disheveled. Ignoring Susan's cry of welcome, he streaked past them and shouldered his way into the library, the door of which was on the latch. Soon they heard protests from within, and Susan ran after him. "That wasn't fair," declared Nick. "He clawed me behind the curtain. *You* wouldn't have found me for a long time." A triumphant Susan reappeared, leading her scowling brother. But when he saw Anabel, his face lit. "Mama, you are home!" He threw himself into her arms.

Susan put her hands on her hips. "Well, of course she's

home. It's nearly dinnertime. Now you must help me find the others before we are made to stop."

Anabel smiled into Nick's eyes and caressed his soft brown hair. "There is nothing wrong," she said.

Nick swallowed, then looked at Hanford.

"For dinner," Christopher said. "I promised, remember?" The boy nodded, blinking rapidly.

"Come *on*," said Susan, starting up the stairs again. "Daisy's here."

The cat had indeed emerged, and Susan was trying to carry him, very much against his inclination. Nick hesitated. "Go ahead," said Anabel. "I must change." They walked up together, and Anabel parted from the others at the drawing-room doorway. She was eager to wash the dust from her face and hands, and exchange her crumpled morning dress for a fresh gown.

She did not linger in her bedroom, however. In a quarter hour she was down again to find the drawing room empty. Puzzled, she walked to the stairs and looked down. No one was about. What had become of them? As she walked back down the corridor Christopher suddenly peered out of the back parlor, them emerged to join her. "I have been recruited into the game," he said, smiling. "I thought to end it, but Susan was very insistent. So I offered to be the seeker. I meant to find your mother and Georgina, and give them the news." He shrugged, smiling wryly. "But I cannot. And now Susan and Nicholas have hidden again, and there has been no sign whatsoever of William."

Anabel laughed. "We will find them together. And then we will announce our plans to everyone. I have an idea where Mama may be."

They found Lady Goring in the small writing closet adjoining her bedchamber, just as Anabel had suspected. She was writing a letter and looked up with slight annoyance when the door opened. But when she saw Anabel, she was on her feet at once and embracing her. "Where have you *been?*"

Anabel explained, her account punctuated by her mother's cries of outrage. "How dare he?" she exclaimed when the story was finished. "I can hardly credit it, even of him."

"It is over now," answered Anabel. "He will not trouble us again. I prefer to think of the future." She smiled at Christopher, and he squeezed her hand. "In fact, Mama, we want to tell the children of our plans. You must help us find them."

"Hide and seek in earnest?" responded Lady Goring with a smile. "Very well. And we will have some champagne with dinner, to celebrate."

"Where do you suppose Georgina has gone?"

Lady Goring shook her head. "She was deep into the game when we separated. She might be anywhere from the attics to the cellars. And the children . . . !" She spread her hands eloquently.

Hanford grinned. "We will start in the attics, then, and move downward, with you guarding the stairs, Lady Goring, to see that no one slips past. We will soon uncover them."

Anabel laughed at him. "You are enjoying this."

"Why not?" He put an arm about her as they started toward the stairs. "I shall enjoy every moment of my life from now on."

Discreetly Lady Goring moved ahead, and she refrained from comment when the others joined her with flushed faces and sheepish smiles.

Georgina was in the attic. She had settled behind two ancient wardrobe trunks, where a dusty window gave just enough light so that she could read a novel. With the increasing darkness, she had to hold it almost at the end of her nose, and she was so absorbed that she did not even hear them approach. Only when Hanford said, "Found!" did she start and look up.

"I didn't think anyone would find me here," she replied, disappointed. Then she saw who it was. "Anabel! Are you . . . that is, we were worried about you."

"All is well," answered her cousin. "Except everyone is hiding. Come and help us find them."

"Did you discover me first?" she said. "I thought I had been so clever."

"We have Lady Goring," Christopher assured her. "And we started at the top of the house."

The rest of the attics were untenanted. On the nursery floor below, they were just about to give up when Anabel remembered a tiny storage room under the stairs. Holding their candles into its dimness, they discovered William crouched among the discarded furniture and linen. He bounced out at once. "Where is Susan? She's supposed to be looking."

"We have taken her place. Come along and help search for her and Nick."

William looked disgusted at being found before them. "Oh, *I* know where Nick will be. Behind the curtain in the library; he always hides there."

"I think he has left it for another spot," replied Christopher with a smile. "Daisy routed him."

"Truly?" The boy laughed. "How he hates that cat. If he would but ignore it, it wouldn't torment him so."

The adults exchanged a smile at this bit of wisdom.

"He is probably in the kitchens, then. Once, when we were playing, he hid there eating cake the whole time!" He frowned. "Why didn't I remember that before? I'm hungry."

"It is nearly dinnertime," said Anabel. "We will eat as soon as we find the others."

William started forward. "I'll look in the kitchen."

Christopher caught him. "No, we will stay with our system. First, the drawing-room floor."

There was no one there; nor did they discover Nick or Susan on the ground floor. "They must have gone to the cellars," marveled William. "I should think Susan would be frightened."

Taking a large branch of candles, all but Lady Goring descended the cellar stairs. The foundations of the house were a vast, echoing space supported here and there by a stone pillar and piled with stores.

"Nick! Susan!" called William. "Come out."

There was no response.

"They mean to make us find them," he added, disgusted.

"Do come out," urged Anabel. "It is nearly dinnertime, and we have something to tell you."

In the far corner of the cellar, Nick's head appeared from behind a pile of boxes. He was very dirty. "All right," he responded, moving toward them.

"Where is Susan?" asked his mother.

"*I* don't know. Hiding with her wretched cat, I suppose."

"Didn't you come down here together?"

"No. I went back into the library." Here William made a small triumphant sound. "But the stupid cat came after me and wouldn't let me be, so I shut it in and tried the cellar."

"Where can she be?" Anabel frowned.

"I didn't see the cat in the library," replied Hanford.

"It wasn't there," agreed Lady Goring. "I *always* notice Daisy."

"We must have overlooked their hiding place," said Anabel. "We shall have to search again."

Without obvious enthusiasm, the group returned to the ground floor and began to look for Susan. When they had scoured the house yet again, they congregated in the nursery and wondered what to do. It was past dinnertime.

Cook was becoming annoyed, and the rest of them were hungry. The boys favored sitting down to eat and letting Susan take her chances, but Anabel wished to find her first. "I am a little worried," she admitted.

"She is crouching somewhere and laughing at us, Mama," sighed William. "She is so small; she might be anywhere. And if she will not come out when we call her . . ."

"She had to hear us," put in Nicholas. "We shouted in every room."

"Perhaps she is hurt, or . . ."

Both boys gazed at their mother skeptically. They had played such games with Susan often. Anabel hesitated. "Well . . ."

"Let us at least go down to the drawing room," declared Lady Goring, who was looking irritated. "And let us announce dinner. Perhaps that will bring her out." She glanced meaningfully at the boys, who rightly interpreted this as a signal to shout her announcement.

It was thus a very odd descent from the upper floor. William and Nick went first, advertising dinner at the top of their lungs, followed by the older members of the party, looking variously concerned, amused, and annoyed. Their own noise obscured a rising disturbance lower down for quite a while, but finally, in a lull, they heard a confused shouting and thumping from belowstairs. "What is that?" asked Anabel, hushing her sons.

"It sounds as if it is coming from the kitchens," replied Georgina, who was fighting a smile.

"That cat!" exclaimed Lady Goring, picking up her skirts and hurrying down the staircase.

It was not only Daisy. It was Susan, too. The cat was racing round and round the kitchen, claws rasping on the brick floor, ginger fur wild, with one of the kitchen maids in hot pursuit with a cleaver. Susan, her face smeared with a dark substance, was standing before Cook, her head hanging, but when the others burst in and she looked up, a spark of unrepentant mischief gleamed in her green eyes.

"What is happening here?" demanded Lady Goring in a penetrating voice.

The kitchen maid froze, allowing Daisy to escape into the scullery. Susan bit her lower lip, and Cook turned, arms akimbo and scowling, to reply, "Miss Susan was found in the larder, if you please, ma'am, eating the chocolate cake I baked for tea tomorrow. Indeed, she has as good as finished it, and I expect she will be sick now."

Susan shook her head. Her brothers eyed her with half-admiring outrage. "Nick's trick," murmured William.

"Well, she shan't have any dinner, then," said Anabel, moving to take Susan's hand—then shifting to her upper arm when she saw the sticky state of that member. "Come along and get washed."

With a malicious grin at the boys, Susan allowed herself to be led away.

Some twenty minutes later, they were all gathered around the table eating dinner. Anabel had relented and allowed Susan to join them, in view of the momentous news that was to be imparted there, but the girl was not eating. She watched the others devour roast chickens and a ragout of beef with some contempt, and her superior little face caused more than one of the adults to suppress a smile during the course of the meal.

When the servants had brought the last of the dishes and retired to the kitchen, Anabel looked around the table. "We have something to tell you all," she said.

The boys raised their heads, and Susan turned. Under their collective gaze, Anabel quailed a little. The last time she had made such an announcement, the reaction had been far from favorable. And though she knew the children loved Christopher, there was no predicting what they would think. She glanced at him, and he smiled reassuringly.

"Uncle Christopher and I have decided to marry," she finished.

There was a moment's silence. Lady Goring smiled benignly, and Georgina more fixedly. Then the table erupted in shouts of wondering glee, and all the children spoke at once.

"Hurray!" exclaimed William.

"I'm very glad," said Nick.

"Will Uncle Christopher live with us?" asked Susan.

Anabel laughed with relief and happiness. "Yes," said Hanford in reply to this last question, "and you had best beware, young miss, for I shall be a very strict disciplinarian. It was obvious today that you require one."

Susan giggled. "Daisy likes you, too," she answered.

"Does he? I am deeply honored."

"This is wonderful," put in William. "Everything is coming out splendidly just after it seemed that nothing was right."

Anabel sat back, listening to the happy chatter and watching Christopher talk with the children. William was right. She had never felt happier in her life.

When dinner was over and the children had been taken upstairs to bed, Lady Goring and Georgina left the engaged couple alone in the drawing room. They settled on the sofa and let out identical sighs of contentment.

"I'm glad *that* is over," she said.

"Did you really doubt their approval?"

"No, I suppose not. But . . ."

"But you weren't certain they had ever considered me in that light," he finished teasingly.

"Christopher! How can you remind me of my idiocy? I was stupidly blind for so long. It makes me blush with shame."

"Ah, but I mean to extract full payment."

She smiled. "What sort of payment?"

Instead of answering, he bent and kissed her, slowly and gently at first, then more passionately. Anabel felt again that thrill of response through her whole body. She put her arms around his neck and gave herself totally to the embrace.

It was some time before she could speak again, and when she did, she was breathless. "That is the sort of debt I shall never wish to pay off," she murmured.

Christopher's blue eyes shone as he gave the only conceivable answer to this, pulling her close once again.

About the Author

Jane Ashford grew up in the American Midwest. A lifelong love of English literature led her eventually to a doctorate in English and to extensive travel in England. After working as a teacher and an editor, she began to write, drawing on her knowledge of eighteenth- and nineteenth-century history. She now divides her time between New York City and Kent, Connecticut.

Jane Ashford's other Regency Romances— A RADICAL ARRANGEMENT, THE HEADSTRONG WARD, THE MARCHINGTON SCANDAL, THE THREE GRACES—are also available in Signet editions.

Other Regency Romances from SIGNET

*Prices slightly higher in Canada

SIGNET Regency Romances You'll Enjoy

Buy them at your local

bookstore or use coupon

on next page for ordering.